SPYING ON MY SCOUNDREL

SPYING ON MY SCOUNDREL

LINKED ACROSS TIME BOOK 13

DAWN BROWER

For my Family, without you, I'd probably have run out of ideas a long time ago. I might become...crabby from time to time, but I love you. I'm blessed to have you in my life, especially on the darkest of days when their doesn't seem any hope to find any light. Thank you for supporting me. There are not words to tell you how much I appreciate everything you do for me.

The sun itself sees not till heaven clears.

— WILLIAM SHAKESPEARE, SONNET

CONTENTS

DESCRIPTION

Lady Hyacinth believes she's destined to be a princess. The prince of a small country visits London and she declares she'll make him fall in love with her in less than a sennight. After all, she is the most eligible lady in all of England...

Rhys Rossington, the Earl of Carrick works for the home office and he's assigned to the prince while he's visiting. Some believe he is visiting for nefarious reasons and expect Rhys to uncover if the royal visit is something evil in disguise.

Rhys and Hyacinth each have their own reasons for attaching themselves to the prince, but neither one of them expect where it will lead them. They have always hated each other. Whatever differences they had are nothing in the face of danger.

As each moment passes both Rhys and Hyacinth begin to understand the meaning of the saying: There's a fine line between love and hate. If the survive they will have to decide which side their feelings actually fall on...

CHAPTER 1

Summer 1835

Lady Hyacinth Barrington would much rather be home at Havenwood, but instead she stared out the window of her family's carriage. They were headed to Weston Manor for a house party that her mother thought would be good for Hyacinth and her brother, Elijah. None of them liked leaving home, but at least the house party wasn't supposed to be longer than a fortnight. Then they could return home and enjoy the rest of summer unencumbered. That is if their mother didn't accept any more invitations for them.

"How much longer do we have to be in the carriage?" Elijah nearly whined the question out.

Hyacinth couldn't blame him—though, for a boy on the cusp of manhood at ten and six, he sure acted like a spoiled child. She wanted to escape the phaeton too, but she refused to act undignified. Still, it seemed as if they'd been traveling forever.

"Not much longer," their mother answered.

"Is Uncle Killian attending this party too?" Elijah asked. He ran his fingers through his unruly brown hair, making his locks stick out even more at odd angles.

Elijah hero-worshipped their uncle. He followed him around as much as Uncle Killian allowed, which was far more than Hyacinth ever would. She found her brother irritating and would hate it if he went everywhere with her. Another reason she detested the idea of this house party.

"Uncle Killian is not going to attend," their mother, Odessa, the Countess of Havenwood, answered Elijah. She brushed a stray lock of her dark hair behind her ear. It had come unpinned when an unruly breeze whipped through the carriage earlier. "I do believe Scarlett will be there with your Aunt Aubriella."

Hyacinth wrinkled her nose. She liked her cousin, but there was something odd about her. Scarlett could be a little cryptic at times. She would say the strangest things that Hyacinth didn't fully understand. Aunt Aubriella was like that too. It was almost as if they didn't belong, but of course they did. They were family.

"You didn't mention they were going to attend the house party," Hyacinth said. "Why are they not traveling with us?"

What reason could her mother have had to keep that information to herself? Hyacinth stared at her and waited for her to speak, but her mother remained silent. She refused to let it go though. Hyacinth was not going to forget about it anytime soon.

A manor house came into view, and they all turned their attention to it. "Is that Weston?" Elijah asked.

"I believe it is," their mother answered him.

It was a large estate set near large cliffs that dipped down to the ocean below. Hyacinth was intrigued. She'd never been to this part of the country, and while she'd never admit it aloud, she was eager to explore the beach below the cliffs. She'd heard there were caves that led down to the shore. When she had a chance, she'd see for herself if they existed. First, she'd have to make sure Elijah wasn't trailing after her. She wouldn't be responsible for him.

"Mother," Hyacinth said. "About Aunt Aubriella and Scarlett…"

"They will join us later this week," her mother interrupted. "There was an emergency at Kingsbridge, and they couldn't travel with us."

Hyacinth narrowed her gaze. She still believed her mother was holding something back, but she'd let it go. "All right."

Their carriage turned down the long drive and headed toward the front entrance of Weston Manor. Hyacinth stared toward the cliffs. Three young gentlemen were walking together toward the edge. Two were identical twins, Christian Kendall, the Marquess of Blackthorn, and the heir to the Weston dukedom; and Lord Nicholas Kendall, the spare. Hyacinth couldn't be certain, but she assumed the other gentleman with them was their younger cousin, Rhys Rossington, the Earl of Carrick, and heir to the Marquess of Seabrook. Where the twins had dark hair, the young earl had golden blond hair that gleamed in the sunlight. Hyacinth wanted a closer look at him. There was something about him that drew her notice.

She sighed. Hyacinth had turned ten and four a

couple weeks ago. Her birthday celebration had been wonderful. Her father believed in cherishing every moment, and special occasions such as birthdays would always be treasured the most. It was one of the reasons she adored her father. She couldn't imagine not having him in her life, and she hoped she wouldn't have to for many years to come. She really wished he had come with them on this trip.

Still, there could be interesting things to discover. Maybe she should follow the twins and the earl around. They would surely know the best places on the estate, and boys always went where they were not supposed to. Those were the places Hyacinth wanted to uncover. The secret areas... She wanted something exciting and maybe a little dangerous to help her forget that her father had stayed home and she had to suffer at a house party for a whole fortnight.

The carriage came to a stop in front of the house. "Finally," Elijah exclaimed. "I thought we'd never arrive. The ride down the drive felt as if it took an eternity."

Hyacinth rolled her eyes. Her brother could be so dramatic. "Then it's good that we have finally reached the end."

The phaeton came to a stop in front of the house.

A footman opened the door and helped their mother out. Hyacinth followed after her, and Elijah leaped from the carriage before anyone could prevent him. He ran up the stairs and into the house.

"Elijah, wait," her mother called out, but it was to no avail. Elijah was gone.

"He probably went to the kitchen to beg for something to eat," Hyacinth said.

"He doesn't know where the kitchen is," her mother said exasperated.

"He'll find it," Hyacinth replied. "His stomach will lead the way."

Her brother's dramatics far outweighed the amount of food he consumed. They walked into the manor and were greeted by the Duchess of Weston, then showed to their room. Hyacinth had wanted to explore the cliffs, but now that they'd arrived, she was suddenly tired. So instead of finding the twins and the earl, she decided to take a nap. Maybe later she could find them. If she was lucky, they'd willing allow her to tag along with them. Either way, she fully intended to go wherever they went. Whether they liked it or not.

LATER THAT NIGHT...

Rhys stared at the entrance to the caves. Weston Manor was his home away from home. He loved visiting his cousins. It also gave him time to himself, without her constantly annoying him. Charlotte always wanted to trail after him. Unfortunately, she was also visiting during this trip. Lucky for him though, his cousin, Elizabeth, had Charlotte's attention. For now, she would trail after her and leave Rhys to explore the caves on his own.

"Where are you going?"

He closed his eyes and groaned. Rhys thought he'd slipped away unnoticed. He should have paid more attention. Of course, Lady Hyacinth Barrington had followed him out to the cliffs. If there was a female even more annoying than his sister, it was her.

"Isn't there someone else you can bother?" Impatience flooded his voice as he addressed her. "Go away."

Rhys didn't bother to glance back at her. It would give her permission to continue with him as he walked into the caves. He hoped she didn't consider coming in after him, but with Lady Hyacinth, predicting what she might do often proved difficult. There was a chance he'd made a wrong calculation. He prayed he hadn't as he moved farther into the cavern. If he hoped to be as good a spy as his father, Dominic, the Marquess of Seabrook, he had to practice his sneaking around skills. So far they were abysmal…

He stopped a moment to allow his eyesight to adjust to the darkness. Rhys could have brought a candle or a lantern, but had decided against it. A good spy didn't use anything to light their path. That would make them easier to spot, and for the bad people to catch them. He wanted to be the best, and he would.

"Ouch," Lady Hyacinth muttered as she ran into him. "Why did you stop?"

Rhys cursed under his breath. "Why are you still here? I told you to go."

"You're not my father or any male relation I am required to at least pretend to listen to." She jutted her chin out. He could barely make out her features in the dark, but that defiant gesture was unmistakable. "I want to see the caves. It has nothing to do with you."

He had a difficult time believing her. "Is that so?" Rhys lifted a mocking brow. He doubted she could see it, but it was more a reflex than anything. "Then you don't mind me leaving you to fend for yourself then."

"I don't," she replied defiantly.

"Good," he said and left her alone to continue his journey. Hopefully, without her trailing behind him… Something told him he wouldn't be so lucky. Nothing about this excursion had gone right and he didn't expect it to. Though, to be fair, a good spy should be able to compromise and think fast when needed. Nothing ever went how it was supposed to. That was a fact of life.

He finally reached the end of the cavern and stepped out on to the beach. Moonlight streamed over the water as the waves crashed to the shore. He took a deep breath and savored the moment. He'd made it. No light to guide him, and save for Lady Hyacinth, without incident. Rhys turned toward the entrance to the cave and frowned. She should have come out to the beach already. He sighed. She was probably stuck somewhere, and he would have to go in and save her. *Damn her.* Why couldn't she be a normal lady and stay at the manor?

Rhys moved back toward the cavern, and as he was about to step inside, she came tumbling out, knocking him to the ground with her landing on top of him. He struggled to breathe and his chest hurt. "I hate you," he wheezed out. He wrapped his arms around her instinctively to protect her from injury.

"You're a bloody arse," she said. Hyacinth struggled against him and shoved her elbow into his side. It made him groan from the pain she inflicted. "Let me go."

"Sweetness," he said gruffly, "no one is holding you, least of all me."

He was only six and ten. A mere two years her senior, and he shouldn't like anything about her, but he did. He would never admit aloud how pretty he thought her. One day she'd grow into a true beauty. Now though, she was a thorn in his side, his chest to be more precise, and he had to ensure she made it back to the manor unscathed. His family would have his head if anything happened to her. He should have marched her back immediately, but he hadn't wanted to give up on his goals.

"I hate you too," she told him and pushed herself upward.

He groaned as she used him to vault upward. Pain shot through him again. "Glad we can agree on something," he mumbled. "Now that we settled that, we can climb back up and head back to the manor."

She didn't give him a response. There were a few noises, and she may have muttered something under her breath, but it was nonsensical. He really didn't care. Rhys rubbed his chest and came to his feet. He followed behind her as she entered the cavern again. As they moved in silence, he couldn't help being grateful he didn't have to interact with her much. They rarely crossed paths, and he didn't foresee that changing in the future.

They finally reached the top and exited the cave. Lady Hyacinth stomped away from him in a fury. He shook his head and ambled behind her. At least he could be assured she would make it back inside the manor safely. After that, he could go in search of his cousins, Christian and Nicholas. They would probably be in the game room. That is if his father and uncle were not in there. Either way, he would be free of Lady Hyacinth and her histrionics.

She stomped inside and he breathed a sigh of relief. He went in the opposite direction and decided to enter through the garden. Rhys whistled as he walked. All in all, it hadn't been a bad night. He might be able to do this spy business after all.

Ten years later...

yacinth stared at the soft pink silk of her gown and frowned. She wasn't certain she liked the shade, but there were not many colors allowed for unmarried ladies to select from. Pink was one of the more favorable choices. She'd prefer red. A dark, striking, bold cherry gown... One day she'd have one. She'd make sure of it. Hyacinth sighed and stood. She crossed her bedchamber and pulled the door open and found her cousin, Scarlett practically bouncing down the hallway.

"Hy." Scarlett stopped in front of Hyacinth and patted her arm. "Did you hear?"

Scarlett could be high-spirited at times. A hellion

on a good day, something more defiant any other time… She had her mother's red-hair, albeit a couple shades darker, and her father's temper. Lady Scarlett Lynwood had gumption to spare. She read anything and everything, had strange ideas, and didn't have any issue telling the ton exactly what she thought of them. Hyacinth blamed Aunt Aubriella, Scarlett's mother, for that. It could be embarrassing in Scarlett's company at times, but she was family and Hyacinth didn't abandon anyone she cared about.

"What should I have heard?" Scarlett wasn't wearing white or even a soft shade of pink. She was only half a year older than her. How did she get permission to wear dark green?

"Isn't it exciting?" It would be better if they could talk in private. Scarlett's propensity for odd speeches and borderline fortunetelling could be taken the wrong way. They should go downstairs or even back into Hyacinth's bedchamber, but sometimes it was too difficult to corral Scarlett. "A prince is visiting," she squealed out the words.

That actually gained Hyacinth's attention. An actual prince was coming to England? She turned her attention to Scarlett. "Are you certain?" She had to uncover all the pertinent details. If she could somehow catch this prince's notice, and perhaps his ardor, then she could be a princess. She always wanted to be a princess. Well, actually, she wanted to be a duchess. That would never be enough now though. Not since Lady Elizabeth Kendall married the Duke of Whitewood and became a duchess herself. She wanted to have a loftier title than her. Lady Elizabeth had always acted superior, and it vexed Hyacinth to no end. She loathed Lady Elizabeth, and it would be splendid if she could hold herself higher than her in society.

Scarlett nodded her head vigorously. "While I was at the bookstore I overheard a conversation between the Earl of Carrick and the Marquess of Chisenhall. The prince arrived a few days ago, and he's to make his first appearance tonight at the Silverly ball."

"That's fascinating," Hyacinth said in a mixed tone, slightly blasé

and mild interest in a way that only she could master. Was it too much to hope that the Earl of Carrick wouldn't be a part of the prince's entourage? She hated that man… That was the only disconcerting news Scarlett had imparted thus far. She stared at her pink gown, even more frustrated than before. How was she to shine for the prince in such a dull color? She'll have to try. Hyacinth couldn't be certain what might work, but she would worry about that later. "Are you attending the ball tonight then?"

"Indeed," Scarlett said. "It's not every day that a new prince visits. Do you suppose he'll be handsome?"

"I wouldn't know." Though she hoped he proved to be much more handsome than the Duke of Whitewood. That would be another thing she could lord over Lady Elizabeth. She wrinkled her nose. "Not all princes are created equal. Did you overhear any other pertinent details?"

Scarlett shook her head. "Not much… His name is Adrian Ene, the Crown Prince of Vasinova. The earl and marquess moved out of the bookstore and left it impossible for me to hear anything else."

"I suppose we'll have to wait and see at the ball. Has the carriage been called for?" She stepped fully into the hall and started for the stairs. Scarlett would follow along. "It should be time to leave, don't you think?"

At the bottom of the staircase, waited Scarlett's father, Killian, the Earl of Thornbury. "Ah, there the two of you are," he said. "I thought I'd have to go in search of you."

Scarlett giggled. "Father, you worry too much.

We're not late in the least. I didn't realize you would be chaperoning us tonight."

He smiled at her. "Your dear Aunt Odessa is indisposed tonight and begged me to stand in for her. I hope that's all right with you."

"As long as you don't chase all my suitors away." She wrinkled her nose. "Not that I have many."

"Which suits me fine," he said and chuckled. "No man is good enough for my daughter." He turned toward Hyacinth. "Or my niece."

"Thank you for remembering my existence, Uncle Killian," she chastised him. "I'm glad you'll be with us tonight. My mother needs to take better care of herself."

"Then we better be off," he said. "So she doesn't have time to reconsider her decision to stay in. Hurry out the door and in the carriage now." He shooed them both through the foyer.

The trek to the Silverly ball wasn't a long one; however, the line of carriages delayed entrance by at least an hour. Hyacinth didn't usually mind because she liked being fashionably late. The more people in the ballroom when she was announced the better. Tonight though, she wanted inside as soon as possible. She wanted to sneak a glance at the prince.

"This is taking too long," Scarlett whined.

"Are you regretting your decision to attend the ball?" Hyacinth raised a brow. "This's normal. You do remember that, do you not?" Of course, she was equally impatient, but she'd never admit that aloud. She could encourage Scarlett's bad behavior. It might help her get inside faster.

"I didn't forget," Scarlett sneered. "That doesn't mean I like it."

They finally reached the entrance. A footman opened the carriage door and assisted Hyacinth and Scarlett down. Uncle Killian followed after. They went inside and waited for one of the servants to announce them. When they entered the ballroom, it was almost at full capacity. The entire ton must have decided to attend the Silverly ball. The news had gone widespread regarding the Prince's arrival. That could be the only explanation for the large crowd.

"Are you actually going to dance?" she asked Scarlett. "Or are you going to hug the wall tonight?"

"I actually thought I might spend some time in the card room," she retorted. "There is more interesting conversation in there, and I might find someone worth spending time with."

"You'll do nothing of the sort," her father ordered. "You'll stay in this ballroom the entire night or we're going home this second."

Hyacinth held back a smile. This was why she had been glad her uncle agreed to chaperone them instead of her mother. He would be solely focused on Scarlett and Hyacinth could do whatever she pleased. For once, their roles would be reversed.

"Don't worry Uncle Killian," Hyacinth said and smiled serenely at him. "Scarlett wouldn't dare disappoint you."

Her cousin glared at her and then at her father. "You're both awful." She probably would have stomped her foot in defiance if they were at home. Even Scarlett had limits. "Fine. I'll dance. But I refuse to like it."

"As long as we understand each other."

Hyacinth fought back laughter. "I'll leave you two to your discussion. I'm going to get something to drink from the refreshment table and find a few gentlemen to sign my dance card."

She slipped away before either one of them could stop her. Hyacinth had a purpose, and she would not allow anything to prevent her from finding the prince. Of course, she had no inkling of what he looked like, but it shouldn't be difficult to discern his identity. Hyacinth was acquainted with most of the members of the ton. So, in theory, she should be able to locate him based on the fact he'd be one of the few individuals at the ball she didn't actually know. There may be a few holes in that notion, but it was all she had.

Hyacinth circled the ballroom, but she didn't catch sight of the prince. Frustration grew inside of her. Perhaps he hadn't arrived yet, or he may have gone outside to the garden for a bit of fresh air. She had checked every other possible location, so why not go outside. It was a little chilly for spring weather, but not horribly so.

She slipped out the doors leading to the terrace and stared up. Stars glittered the dark sky like diamonds on velvet. Briefly mesmerized by the sheer beauty of it, Hyacinth shook off the fleeting moment. She didn't have time for wistfulness or anything that might distract her. Hyacinth strolled along the balcony until she reached a set of stairs that led toward the garden.

The only light guiding her path came from the full moon overhead. It was enough, or at least she hoped. She stumbled a little down the steps and reached for the railing to keep from falling. Her foot slipped on the bottom step, and she fell forward, hitting the ground hard. She cursed under her breath.

Her palms stung from the tiny pebbles that were

all over the stone path. She rubbed her hands together to try to ease the pain. "My luck would be like this," Hyacinth grumbled. "This is what I get searching for a prince to swoop in and save me. I don't know why I bother."

"Who's there?" a man asked.

Hyacinth glanced toward the sound. The last thing she wanted was to be discovered in her current predicament. She scrambled to her feet and rushed to hide behind a nearby bush. The gentleman who'd called out, or she presumed it was the same one, came a little closer and glanced around. He seemed to accept that no one was around. Hyacinth took a deep breath and held it until he headed back in the direction he'd come from. She blew it out slowly, but started to panic when he stopped. Another gentleman joined him.

"It must be voices carrying from the ball," he said.

"Are you certain, Marius?" his companion asked. Both of them spoke in an accent Hyacinth didn't recognize. Could they both be from Vasinova? Perhaps one of them was the prince. Excitement filled her. She couldn't reveal herself to them now though. How would that look? The prince would never consider her as a potential wife if she was seen frolicking in bushes at a ball.

"As certain as I can be, Your Highness," Marius answered.

It *was* the prince! She could barely conceal her delight. If only she dared to sneak a glance. At least she had some proximity to him. Eavesdropping on their conversation might prove useful in her endeavor.

"Very well," the prince said. "But to be safe, perhaps we should continue our conversation in a more private location."

"You're right, of course," Marius agreed. "This visit to England is too important to misstep now. We should mingle a little more with their high society. It'll help conceal our true purpose."

What did he mean by that? Hyacinth couldn't fathom what their actual intent might be, and she wasn't certain she cared. None of that mattered to what she truly desired. She would be a princess.

The men walked away and headed back into the ballroom. Once she was certain they had gone back inside, she slipped out from the bushes. Her dress and hair must be a fright. She would have to sneak into the ladies' retiring room and repair the damage.

She strolled toward the stairs and ran smack into a hard male chest. Hyacinth stumbled backward, but he caught her before she could hit the ground, again.

"Lady Hyacinth," the gentleman said with a hint of displeasure in his tone. "What the are you scheming now?"

Hyacinth groaned. Of course *he* would be the one to catch her. Not that she'd have fallen in the first place, if not for him stepping in front of her. She really hated Rhys Rossington, the Earl of Carrick. He was the bane of her existence...

CHAPTER 3

Rhys had been trailing behind the prince and his secretary at a discreet distance. They hadn't said enough for him to garner what their plan was, but he did discover they indeed had one. This state visit had been scheduled unexpectedly and deemed suspicious by the home office. Rhys was still considered inexperienced, but his status in the *ton* gave him more reach then many home office members. He'd won the assignment by default.

He'd been doing decent with it too…until Lady Hyacinth Barrington decided to leave the ballroom for her own private tour of the gardens. He'd been secretly fuming at her for the past few minutes. At least she had the good sense to hide in the bushes and not throw herself at the prince. That would not have been good for her, or Rhys. He had to wonder though what had made her think going into the garden alone was anywhere near a proper notion for her.

Lady Hyacinth pushed her lips together into a firm line and glared at him. "I could ask you the same thing," she retorted. "Why are you skulking in the shadows?"

As if he'd tell her… "It's perfectly acceptable for a gentleman to be alone in the garden. A lady; however, should not be unaccompanied."

Somehow, he didn't think that would settle well with Lady Hyacinth. She had always been a bit… high on the instep. Rhys fully expected her to be difficult.

"You're the worst…" She stomped her foot. "I don't need any lectures. Especially from you."

"You need something." What she needed was a good spanking. Though she might enjoy that. Something told him she had a few eccentricities, and that appealed to him more than he wanted to admit even to himself. "But I won't stand out here discussing it with you. It's time for you to go inside and behave like a good lady should."

Lady Hyacinth clenched her hands together into

tight fists at her sides. Did she plan on hitting him? That would be interesting. Still, it was not the time to test her patience. His was already straddling a very thin line. Rhys shouldn't be amused, but he couldn't help himself. A twisted side of him had always enjoyed her spirited side. "I find it interesting that you deflected earlier. Instead of answering my question, you turned everything back on me."

"I don't believe I understand what you're implying." He'd hoped she would forget her earlier inquisitiveness. "I believe I addressed your unnecessary concerns."

"You did nothing of the sort." She turned her nose up. "All you've done is chastise me for daring to be outside alone. It's ridiculous that, because I am a woman, I cannot do as I please."

"Your opinion in this matters not." He took a step toward her. "What does is the fact you *are* a woman, and society has far different expectations for you than a gentleman. Accept it as any other lady in your station has, and you'll be far happier."

He didn't subscribe to those notions himself. His Aunt Alys would have his head if she overheard him now, and his mother would help her. He didn't even want to think about what his sister, Charlotte, or his cousin, Elizabeth, might do. There were too many strong-willed females in his family to knock heads with. He didn't owe Lady Hyacinth the same considerations as he did his family. If she insisted on putting herself in dangerous situations, it was his duty to show her the error of her ways.

She rolled her eyes. There was very little light shining from the moon but her action proved unmistakable. "You know nothing of what might constitute happiness for me. Quit with the condescending lecture as if you have any way of discerning *my* truth. Go back inside and find an insipid young miss to tote your beliefs on. They *might* consider your every word worth listening to. *I* know better."

"Please," he began. "Don't be a fool. You may actually believe you have a modicum of understanding, but I think it's time you're honest with yourself." He stepped even closer to her. "You are good at speeches and spectacular dressing downs, but you have no inkling about anything real." She exhaled audibly as if offended by his statement. Her cheeks flushed a nice shade of red, slightly visible in the moonlight. He may not have noticed if they had more distance between them... Her heat mixed with his, and he almost gave in and kissed her; he held back by sheer will alone.

He continued, because she had to hear everything

he had to say, "You're a pampered princess who rarely comes down from her tower to mix company with the plebeians beneath you. Happiness is as trivial as your silk gown and lace trimming. Even your dainty pearl necklace and earbobs are nothing but pretense." He lightly flicked the pearl and diamond earring dangling from her left ear with his index finger. "You, sweetness, are as shallow as all those young misses you consider unsophisticated and unworthy." He moved his hand over and brushed his knuckles against her cheek. "Besides... you *do* listen to me. Otherwise, you would have left the moment you saw me. Admit it, Lady Hyacinth, you *like* me."

He was probably pushing her too far. She should stop him before he took things in a direction they both might regret. What the hell was wrong with him? Why did he want this lady? She drove him senseless on a good day. Anything permanent between them might drive them to interminable insanity.

How dare he... She should slap him. Why wasn't she slapping him? The touch of his hand against her cheek sent shivers down her spine. Her breath hitched a little, and she opened her mouth. No words formed in her mind, and she barely held in a gasp. She had to take a stand…make him understand he had no power over her. Hyacinth intended to marry a prince, and he had no chance of ever raising himself to that high of title. He was a mere earl who would one day be a marquess. She wanted better. It was time to do as he said and leave. She lifted a brow and smirked. "You wish."

"Pardon me?" He tilted his head to the side. "I'm afraid you have me at a loss. I wish what?"

"You are the one who…how did you say it? Like?" She twisted her lips upward into a devious smile. "I'm not so certain that's a strong enough word. You want me to desire you." She closed what little distance there was between them. "Then you could take advantage of little ole naïve me and…" She moved her head so her lips were mere inches from his. "Kiss me." It would be so easy to find out what a kiss would be like between them. He wasn't stepping away. His breathing was more ragged than hers, but her heart had started to beat heavily inside her chest. What the hell was wrong with her? Her body had grown warm, and she found she wanted to kiss him. Hyacinth had to put some distance between them and fast. Playing with fire sounded good in theory, in practice, it fast became ill advised.

"Stop," he said, his voice gruff. "You don't know what you're doing."

In that respect, he was correct. She'd gone in for the kill, in a sense, and she'd bitten off more than she could handle. "Am I bothering you?" He'd challenged her, and she now found herself unable to be the one to back down. Part of her hoped he would cave and give them both what they wanted. One kiss… How much damage could it do?

Lord Carrick groaned. It made every part of her stand on notice. He was about to kiss her. She could feel it deep down to her bones, and she wanted it. Hyacinth had never craved anything as she did her mouth on his. She was inexperienced with kissing. Not that she hadn't been kissed, but the boy who had dared before had been inept. Something told her that Lord Carrick would not be.

"Rhys, are you out here?" a man called out.

They separated as if a bucket of cold water had been tossed over them, alleviating their heated skin. She should thank whoever had interrupted them. Kissing Lord Carrick was an incredibly bad idea. Hyacinth wanted to catch the prince's attention, not the earl's. He didn't deserve her, and she desperately desired to be more than a mere countess.

Lord Carrick continued to stare at Hyacinth as if he wasn't certain what to make of her. His gaze didn't leave hers as he answered, "I'm over here, Christian."

His cousin, the Marquess of Blackthorn… He'd be a better option than Lord Carrick. Though he came with one downside—his sister, Elizabeth. She'd hate to have to socialize with her more often because she had the bad sense to marry her brother.

"You should go before he joins us," Lord Carrick told her.

"Why?" She lifted a brow. "Surely he won't believe anything untoward is happening between us." Hyacinth and Lord Carrick had always been cross with each other. They could not be in each other's company without exchanging words of displeasure. They made no secret that they loathed each other.

The muscles in his jaw clenched and he closed his eyes. Lord Carrick took several breaths and muttered something she couldn't quite hear. Though she suspected he was cursing her very existence. "No," he said. "He wouldn't. But it still looks compromising, and I don't think you'd want to find yourself tethered to me the rest of your days. I assure you, I do not want to find myself your husband in a few short weeks because your stubbornness gave us little choice."

She jutted her chin out. "You're correct. Being married to you would be the worst fate I could possibly imagine. But it's too late to go inside another way. I'll have to hide."

Lord Carrick sighed. "Later we will discuss your spying habits. They will be your undoing one day."

Had he learned nothing? He should know better than to try to convince her of anything. She was perverse enough to do the exact opposite of what he suggested because he was the one doing the advising. Perhaps she should remind him of that fact. "You can try to dissuade me from my proclivities but your words will fall on deaf ears. I'll always do what I want."

"Fine," he said through clenched teeth. "You are one strange lady. If I didn't know better, I'd swear..." Lord Carrick clamped his mouth shut and shook his head. "Never mind that. Go hide in your favorite bush until I lead Christian away. Then go find a ladies' retiring room and fix yourself. You're completely disheveled, and no one will believe you've not been ravished by a scoundrel."

"No scoundrel would risk touching me," she spat at him. "Besides, you're the only gentleman of that caliber I'm acquainted with, and we both know how much you despise me."

He lifted his hand to his forehead and saluted her. "You are indeed correct, sweetness. Now go hide before we're both ruined."

She huffed but did as he instructed. Not because she had any inclination to listen to his orders, but she did agree with him on this one. A marriage between them would be most undesirable, even if she still wondered what a kiss from him might be like. It was a foolish curiosity she would try her best to forget. Lord Carrick wasn't for her. This new prince…he was the prize, and she intended to win it from all the other eligible ladies.

"Why are you hiding out here?" Lord Blackthorn asked.

At first, she thought he saw her in the bushes, but she peeked out and realized his attention was completely on Lord Carrick. "I needed some air." He went to the stairs to join the marquess. "I think it's time I went inside though."

"Your sister is looking for you," Lord Blackthorn said. His voice was laced with a weariness that belied his nonchalant expression. What could be bothering the marquess?

Lord Carrick groaned. "I'm afraid to discover why. I suppose I should find her and deal with her straightaway. Walk with me and tell me what Nicholas had been scheming."

It occurred to her then Lord Carrick never told her why he'd been in the garden. Had he been spying on the prince, too? No. He was probably meeting a married lady or some other woman of loose morals for an assignation. He was a complete rogue, after all. She sighed. Hyacinth was not jealous of this fabricated lady. One he had probably kissed in truth and also liked to be with. Not that she wanted him to kiss her… Except she couldn't help wondering what it might be like to have his lips on hers. To taste him, and have him hold her as if he needed her more than he needed to breathe. Her heart beat rapidly inside her chest and her breathing became ragged.

What was wrong with her?

The two gentlemen moved away from the garden and went back inside. Hyacinth blew out a breath and exited her hiding place. She had a lot to consider, but first she had to go find someplace to make repairs to her dress and hair. Lord Carrick was right. She was a mess.

CHAPTER 4

This was her chance. The prince would be at Lady Kerry's soiree and so would Hyacinth. She'd been unable to gain his notice at the other two social gatherings she'd attended. This may be her last opportunity, and she *would* achieve her goal. Scarlett would attend with her, along with Hyacinth's mother, Lady Havenwood. She hoped her mother would give her a little freedom since the soiree would be more on the informal side.

"Hyacinth, sit up straight. A lady never slouches," Lady Havenwood said. "Scarlett dear, you look lovely. That shade pairs well with your eyes."

Of course it did. It wasn't insipid white with pale pink trimming. Scarlett was wearing a dress the shade of cornflowers that indeed complemented her ice blue eyes. Hyacinth had eyes more the color of sapphires. If they were a lighter shade, her mother might allow her to wear blue too. But no, they had to be dark like the jewel and too dark for a young lady.

Hyacinth wanted to be married. Partly so she could pick her own wardrobe out and wear whatever pleased her. Her mother seemed to nitpick everything. Sometimes, it seemed as if she could do nothing right, and Scarlett remained perfect. "Mother, is father going to join us in London?" At least she could depend on her father to be on her side. Unfortunately, he had to stay at Havenwood and left them alone in London. Elijah had school and escaped their mother's constant criticism even when he was nearby. Hyacinth alone bared the brunt of it.

"I'm afraid he isn't," her mother said quietly. "There was an issue with some of the farming equipment. He cannot leave anytime soon."

Her heart fell. She understood, she did, but it didn't mean she liked it. She missed her father. "How is Elijah?" She had to talk about something, anything, to keep her mother's focus on something other than her. Her brother was finishing his final term at Oxford—which took him longer than it should have to complete. He kept taking more and more classes instead of finalizing his education. If he liked to learn, she might have believed his reason was to gain more knowledge, but Hyacinth didn't believe that malarkey for a second. He went to university to stay away from home more than to gain an education. She often wished she could have attended herself. A higher education was not something a lady sought though. Maybe one day it would be, but for now she had to settle for the life she'd been offered, and sneak several books out of the library at home to read in her room.

Her mother would never approve of her choices there either. Lady Havenwood cared for many things; however, Hyacinth didn't doubt her mother loved her. Her disapproval hurt more than she would ever willingly admit. She could never say anything to her mother because she'd be hurt, and that was the last thing Hyacinth wanted. So she kept the topic of their conversation safe—her brother and father were two safe matters they could discuss without any negative recourse on either side. "Will he join us, or is he going to return to Havenwood with father?"

"I'm not certain what your brother plans," her mother answered. "He hasn't deigned to inform me, and your father didn't mention him in his last correspondence."

There was a hint of pain in her mother's tone as she spoke. As much as she doted on Elijah, she must be upset he'd ignored her of late. "He's a young man on the verge of taking control of his life. I'm sure it's not occurred to him that he should stop and pay his respects to his family." Elijah would take over the Moreland estate soon. Since he was a viscount, mostly an honorary title, he hadn't done much with it. Their father oversaw the smaller property until Elijah was ready to. "Perhaps he will choose to settle down with his responsibilities now. Maybe even take a wife." She doubted he'd consider matrimony, but it would turn Lady Havenwood's attention to something other her, and the many faults she seemingly had. Elijah was twenty and six, he should be more discerning of his future; however, he showed no desire to do anything other than be a wastrel.

"Perhaps," she conceded.

Scarlett scrunched her nose up. "Elijah isn't anywhere near ready to settle down." She laughed. "He has some wildness to tame first. Though I agree he may consider going to Moreland. It's time he did so."

"Have you heard anything from him?" Hyacinth

asked. It made a little bit of sense. Scarlett was close to both her own brother and Elijah. She could be a bit wild herself. A hellion at heart and proud of it…

"No," she said serenely. A far away expression came over her face. As if she saw something no one else did. She did that from time to time. Scarlett could be a bit eerie at times. "It's something I feel deeply though. He will do his part. There's no need to be concerned for him." She placed a hand on Hyacinth's. "You will have love, cousin. When it presents itself to you, don't push it away. Sometimes it comes when you need it the most and expect it the least."

Eerie didn't even begin to describe Scarlett… "Mmhmm." What else was she to say to that? "How will I recognize this love?" she had to ask.

Scarlett shook her head. "It's not for me to say." She shrugged. "I see what I see and cannot always interpret it. Though I can add this little bit: you have already encountered the man of your dreams. It's a matter of time before you both recognize what you mean to each other."

It had to be the prince. He hadn't formally met her and vice versa. That had to be the reason they hadn't uncovered any love between them. The more she thought about it, the more she believed it. This would work. She couldn't wait to arrive at the soiree. Now more than ever she was determined. Scarlett may have obscure visions of sorts, but she had never been wrong. If she believed Hyacinth would find love, she would.

"Very well," Hyacinth said. "I'll remain open to the possibility of love." She would hug her cousin, but it might seem odd in the carriage. Besides, there was only one man she thought she could truly give her heart to, and he didn't seem interested. So she'd settle for a title. Sometimes love wasn't in the cards, and Hyacinth accepted that a long time ago.

Her mother frowned at her from the other side. "Love is important and I do hope you love the man you marry. It's something worth waiting for."

Hyacinth never doubted her parents loved each other. It was evident when they were around each other. Of course she would wish her daughter had love. Hyacinth relaxed against the carriage and closed her eyes. There was not much else to say, and she wanted to be her best when she met the prince.

RHYS STARED AT THE PEOPLE GATHERED AT LADY Kerry's soiree. There were far more ladies and gentlemen in attendance than he expected. Why did they all decide to accept this particular invitation? Adrian Ene, the Crown Prince of Vasinova, must be the reason for the crush. It was certainly the reason Rhys had opted to attend. He'd much rather be in his townhouse or club sipping brandy instead of the warm lemonade the hostess had to offer her guests.

"This is the second event you've attended," Christian said as he came to stand beside him. "Are you ready to settle down or is there some other reason for this increase in social activity?"

He should have considered that line of questioning would be directed at him. "No more than you are," he retorted, then stopped to glance at his cousin. Perhaps he had it all wrong where Christian was concerned as well. "Please tell me you're not looking for a potential wife."

"Not yet," Christian replied smoothly. "I'm at a loss lately. With Nicholas gone I find myself unable to be at ease. It's as if I lost a part of myself when he decided to go on his grand adventure."

Rhys hadn't realized Nicholas was no longer in England. "Where did he go?" When did he leave? He'd absentmindedly asked Christian how Nicholas was doing at the ball the other night, but clearly he hadn't stopped to listen.

"He's gone some place you will not be able to go, and I'm not certain even I could follow. Elizabeth probably could…" He had a stricken expression on his face. "He's gone to the future. To Mother's time."

That hit him in the gut. Christian's mother, Alys, the Duchess of Weston, was a time traveler. It wasn't a secret in the family, but they didn't openly discuss it either. Society wouldn't look at her the same, and most of them wouldn't believe any of it, would probably consider them touched in the head. They accepted she was an American and didn't like that. "I don't understand. Why would he do that?"

Christian shrugged. "Nicholas has never been satisfied with his life. He has no purpose. I suppose this is his way of uncovering one. Somehow, I do not believe we will ever see him again."

"You could be right." It was a lot to absorb. "He will be missed."

"He will," Christian agreed. "So you understand why I'm here. I need to find my own way without my twin."

Rhys nodded. He couldn't recall a time when Christian and Nicholas were not together. It was odd to not have Nicholas around any longer, but they'd adjust in time. He hoped Nicholas would return one day. His absence would be noticed at some juncture, and they would have to figure out how to explain it. "I'm here for you if you need me." He patted Christian on the shoulder. "We will have to go to the club when we leave. I suspect we are both going to need several glasses of brandy."

Lady Hyacinth was at the soiree. He'd noticed her arrival immediately. Now she had given him another reason to be upset. She was flitting around in the prince's vicinity. Did she honestly think she'd gain the man's attention? She had always had high aspirations, and she couldn't get much higher than marrying a prince who would one day be king. He would not admit how much that irritated him.

"I'll hold you to that," Christian answered. He frowned in Lady Hyacinth's direction, but Rhys didn't think she was the reason for his displeasure. His attention seemed to be more on her cousin than Lady Hyacinth. Did Christian have feelings for Lady Scarlett Lynwood? That was interesting…Was there something between the two of them? Christian didn't seem to want to settle down, but perhaps he'd judged the situation incorrectly. Perhaps he'd make some discreet inquiries later.

"If you'll pardon me," Rhys said. "I've been tasked with seeing to the needs of Prince Adrian." He wrinkled his nose in distaste. "He's not very pleasant, but

I must see to my duty." Sometimes he wondered if being a spy was really what he wanted. He'd set himself on this path, and he'd see it through to the end.

He nodded, but his gaze hadn't deviated from Lady Scarlett. Maybe he did have feelings for her. Rhys would have to inquire later. Christian turned his attention to Rhys. "I didn't realize you were working outside of the office. Are they trusting you with more now?"

"They are," he said. Simplicity was the best. He wasn't certain his father would appreciate his new status with the home office. The Marquess of Seabrook didn't want his only son working as a spy of any sort. It didn't matter that his father had been one of the best once upon a time. Rhys was to learn estate management and nothing else. "But it's diplomatic work. There's very little danger involved."

Christian nodded. "Glad you'll stay safe. I'll meet up with you later." He walked away and in the direction of Lady Scarlett. *Definitely something there...*

Rhys shook his head but stopped short when he noticed someone else. What was Sebastian Bennet, the Marquess of Chisenhall, doing there? Was he ensuring Rhys did the task assigned to him? Rhys cursed under his breath. He would not give the Duke of Branterberry a reason to remove him from watching over the prince. If his son, Sebastian, found fault with his work, the duke wouldn't think twice about reassigning him.

Lady Hyacinth was directly in front of the prince now. Rhys wanted to yank her back and order her to find some other gentleman to pursue. He understood that would be the worst thing he could possibly do. She was stubborn. He'd be far better off endorsing her pursuit of the prince. Maybe then she'd do the exact opposite. What was it about her that he found both irresistible and irritating at the same time? He was drawn to her, and he wished, more often than he liked to admit, that he could rid himself of his fixation.

His heart beat heavily inside his chest. She looked lovely and almost innocent. The white gown made her skin glow, and the pink made her seem even more delicate. She was spirited, and that gown gave a man the wrong impression of her. Lady Hyacinth was fiery, passionate, and everything Rhys ever desired, but didn't dare try to gain. He wasn't ready to settle down, and she deserved a man that could give her all of himself. Half of him wanted to beg her to be his, that half would always be hers, but the rest of him needed to pretend he didn't have any feelings at all. He shook it off and closed the distance between them. Rhys had to forget about Lady Hyacinth. The prince was his reason for being at the soiree, not her. Maybe if he reminded himself enough, he might believe it...

CHAPTER 5

The prince was even more gorgeous up close. His eyes were a mesmerizing dark blue that Hyacinth could easily lose herself in. He would make the perfect husband, and she couldn't wait until he realized she'd make the best wife for him. She prayed he would come to that conclusion before he left England. If she kept telling herself all of that she might actually believe it too… She'd spent time with him on several occasions, and she wasn't certain she even liked him. His sole appeal was his title.

Hyacinth didn't know how long his visit would be, but she would ensure she would attempt to endear herself to him before he left. She finally had his attention, and she would not lose it now. Not for anything… She wanted to be a princess, and nothing would stand in her way—not even her own mercurial feelings.

"Lady Hyacinth," the prince began, "you're quite lovely. Gazing upon your beauty makes me question my reluctance to visit your wonderful country before now."

He said the prettiest things… It seemed so simple in a lot of ways. She was aware of her looks, and while she wasn't ugly, to have a man spout flowery words upon meeting her? That seemed off. Most gentleman stayed to safer subjects that would still flatter while not overstating something she didn't actually have—like true beauty. She wasn't about to let this opportunity go though. Whatever his reasons, she fully intended to use them to her advantage. "Thank you, Your Highness," she said softly. "May I ask why you were reluctant to visit?"

There had to be better conversation other than her overstated beauty. She was loath to say it, but the prince was…a bore. Her mind kept wandering to other things, and people, a certain handsome earl to be more precise. She couldn't shake Lord Carrick from her mind. Every so often, she'd glance around hoping to catch a glimpse of his long golden locks. So far, he hadn't made an appearance.

She couldn't be certain if she was disappointed or relieved.

"I despise travel," he said and waved his hand dismissively. "It is quite tedious."

Much like this conversation. Hyacinth wanted to be a princess. She craved what that title would bring her, but she wasn't so sure the cost would be worth it. If she married the prince, she'd have to spend time with him. Share his bed… Pretend to like him… She shook those thoughts away. No man was perfect, and it was foolish of her to think she might find a better option. The prince was the man she coveted. She didn't have to love him, or even like him. His title was what she wanted from him, and she'd pay whatever price she had to.

She'd be a princess.

"I quite agree," she said earnestly. "I've never enjoyed travel myself. If given the choice, I'd never leave home."

"Precisely," Prince Adrian said in a pleased tone. "This trip was essential, or I'd have remained in Vasinova. Perhaps, one day, you'll visit my tiny nation and I can show you what I love about it."

Her heart lurched a little. That was the hitch in her plan. If she married the prince, she'd have to leave England. It hadn't hit her until that moment.

Would she be all right in another country? Could she leave home and never return? Not that the prince had offered her marriage—yet—but if he did, could she say yes and mean it?

When she married Havenwood would no longer be her home. She'd be forced to move to her husband's residence. Prince Adrian lived in an entirely different country. Even visiting Havenwood might prove difficult. It hadn't occurred to her that she might not be able to return to her childhood home if she married the prince. He said he didn't like traveling. Was never seeing Havenwood again worth having the title of princess? Yes, it was. She could recover from the loss of Havenwood. Ending up a spinster with no title was a fate she didn't want to live with. She'd continue her pursuit of the prince.

"If I find myself traveling, I'd be happy to visit your country." Did the prince miss the irony of this conversation? She had agreed she didn't particularly enjoy traveling. Still, he felt the need to tell her to visit his country. Perhaps it was a test of some sort. He may find her appealing, and this was his way of gauging her interest in him. She didn't want to get over excited. The whole conversation could mean nothing since they had recently been formally introduced. He was unlikely to go down on one knee and beg for her to marry him after one conversation.

"Wonderful," he beamed. "Tell me, Lady Hyacinth, do they intend to have dancing at this gathering?"

She wished. At least dancing would be entertaining. "I'm afraid not, Your Highness." Hyacinth smiled serenely or as much as she was able to. She needed to go for a walk. Preferably alone… "Dancing is saved for balls. I'm not certain Lady Kerry has even engaged musicians for this soiree."

"Ah," he said absentmindedly. The prince glanced around the area and seemed to have lost all interest in their conversation. "That is a pity. I'd have loved dancing with you."

"It would have indeed been a pleasure," she said. Hyacinth barely refrained from rolling her eyes. She had to ask herself if she really wanted to be a princess. Prince Adrian was gorgeous, but she couldn't find anything else to admire about him. Later, she'd consider it all again. Perhaps she wasn't being fair to the prince. He might have more depth… somewhere. "I've always enjoyed dancing."

"Perhaps you'll save a dance for me at the next ball." He smiled at her. Something about the prince was off. Hyacinth couldn't say what; however, she swore she could feel it. It was probably her imagination. "I have enjoyed all the entertainments thus far on my visit, and I'd like to become more acquainted with you."

This was everything she wanted, so why did it make her feel empty? "I'll write your name on my dance card once I arrive. What ball are you attending next?" She would have to make sure she would be there. Maybe at the ball she'd feel differently about the prince.

"I'm not certain." He turned to a man nearby. "Marius, what ball will we be attending next?"

"There are no more balls, Your Highness," the man answered. His dark hair was cropped shorter on the sides and slicked back on top. Marius stood completely still as if he feared moving might disrupt his carefully crafted ensemble. Nothing was out of place, and it seemed like he would find it irritating to be entangled in anything...shambolic. "We're to attend a house party at Weston Manor for the next fortnight. We leave at dawn to start our travels."

Hyacinth frowned. A house party at Weston? She held back a sigh. She had some horrid memories from the last house party she attended there. Though the caves along the cliffs were interesting. Perhaps she'd take the time to explore those again.

After all, she had received an invitation to the Weston House party, but had planned on refusing. "Brilliant," she said and smiled brightly. "I'm sure the duchess will plan at least one ball. I'll be at the house party as well."

She would have to remember to reply to the invite when she returned home. Her mother would be pleased she'd decided to attend. She had been advocating for it since the invite had arrived. She let her mind wander and plan. The prince didn't say anything she had to answer specifically anyway. He accepted an occasional nod of the head and kept talking. A sign that life with him would be tedious at best… She'd be a princess though. Wasn't that worth whatever suffering she would have to endure?

RHYS GRITTED HIS TEETH. HE WANTED TO YANK LADY Hyacinth away from the prince's side. How could she stand listening to him blather on and on about nothing? At least he had gained something insightful from the dull conversation: the prince was going to Weston. He suspected there might be a reason for Prince Adrian's visit, and he'd uncover the truth at Weston. He'd grown up exploring the Weston grounds. The only estate he knew better was Seabrook, his home.

"If you'll pardon me, Your Highness," Lady Hyacinth began. "I must speak with my cousin. I look forward to our dance at Weston." She curtsied and walked off before the prince could respond.

Rhys should stay and listen to the prince and his manservant, but he had an urge to follow Lady Hyacinth, and that irritated him far more than he liked to admit. He couldn't leave well enough alone. She moved through the crowd and broke away from them. Her pace was fast until she reached the edge of the garden. She stopped at a fountain and crossed her arms over her chest. Lady Hyacinth rubbed her arms with her hands as if trying to remove a chill. Rhys moved closer to her, keeping his steps as quiet as possible. He didn't want to startle her.

She closed her eyes and lifted her face toward the sky. The sunlight flowed over her and her cheeks had pinkened a little from the bite of the wind. "Are you cold?" he asked.

Lady Hyacinth opened her eyes and frowned at him. "You really need to quit sneaking up on me. It's not very becoming."

"Perhaps," he said noncommittally. "It is not my intention to sneak anywhere." Not entirely the truth.

He'd been practicing that particular skill for years. "But you didn't answer my question. Are you cold?"

"And if I am?" She lifted a brow. "What will you do? Offer me your jacket?" Sometimes she hated Lord Carrick. Other times, she wanted something from him he didn't seem capable of giving her. He had an honorable streak he couldn't ignore. While she might have other feelings for him, that did not mean he returned them.

"If need be," he said. What was it about this woman that made his blood stir? He wanted her as he never craved another. "Would you like for me to offer it to you?"

In another life, he'd offer her far more than his jacket. He should be courting her and securing her hand in marriage. He was done fighting a truth he'd always known. His feelings for her had always been there, but he'd been too afraid to face them. Seeing her with the prince changed everything for him. If he were to marry, she was the only lady that would do for him. He had no plans of tying himself down in wedded bliss. At least not for many, many more years to come. He had to prove something to himself. Until he managed to do that, he couldn't— wouldn't—marry. Oh, but how he wanted her.

"No," she said softly. "I don't want you to feel

obligated to offer me anything."

What did she mean by that. "Be that as it may…" He slid his coat off and placed it over her shoulder. "What kind of gentleman would I be if I refused to aid a lady in need."

She pulled the jacket tighter around her. He knew she'd been cold. "Thank you," Lady Hyacinth said. Her tone remained light, but there was something almost uneasy in it too. He wanted to ask her what was bothering her but didn't feel he had the right.

"It's my pleasure." He tilted his head to the side. He needed to continue the conversation. Unfortunately, he was at a loss for words. This happened sometimes with her. If they were not arguing, they stood together in silence.

"Why are you being nice to me?" She met his gaze boldly; surprise echoed through her voice. "Most days you lecture me as if I were a child. Have you found nothing at fault with me today?"

"It is a rare day that I ever find fault with you." He stepped closer to her and brushed a stray lock behind her ear. "I'm sorry if I ever made you feel less. It's only I wish the best for you and fear you may never have it."

He was turning sentimental. Rhys shouldn't be

talking this way with her, but he couldn't stop the maudlin words from slipping off his tongue. To him, she would always be perfect. Even when she consistently drove him to the brink of insanity…

She snorted. "I don't know why you feel the need to say such nice words to me, but please don't. I am all right with the status of our relationship. At least with you I know exactly what to expect." She slid the jacket off and held it before him. "You've always been honest with me. Don't stop now."

He frowned. "I'm still being truthful." Rhys stared at the jacket in her hands. "Sweetness…" He swallowed the lump in his throat. Rhys wanted to pull her into his arms. To kiss her, comfort her, and declare to her what he truly felt. Somehow, he didn't think she'd appreciate it. For some unknown reason she thought the prince would make a good husband. She kept chasing after him. He'd noticed it straightaway and hadn't liked it one bit.

She shook her head. "Take it. I promise I'll be all right. I'm going to search for my mother and Scarlett. It's time I returned home."

Rhys took the coat and slid it back on. Lady Hyacinth brushed past him and went in search of her family. He wasn't certain what had happened between them. His entire core was shaken.

CHAPTER 6

Hyacinth stared out the carriage window as they traveled down the long drive that led to Weston Manor. In some ways, it was surreal. During the last visit, she'd been nothing more than a child. That was ten years ago. Part of her related to her younger self more than she'd like to admit. That girl had wanted to go home and see her father. That part hadn't changed. It didn't matter if she became a princess in truth; her father always considered her one. In her father's eyes, she could do no wrong. There was something comforting in that.

But there was no going home...and it hurt to accept that.

She had to keep moving forward and uncover what she truly wanted. Coming to this house party was supposed to answer all of her questions once and for all. Hyacinth thought she understood her heart's desire. Now though… She had never been more confused. The next fortnight should help her decide. At least, she hoped so.

"I know I've said this already," her mother began. "But I truly am glad you've decided to attend the house party. It will be your last chance to secure a match before we retire to the country."

"Perhaps I'm doomed to remain an old maid," Hyacinth said bitterly. "It may be for the best. I prefer Havenwood anyway. I'm sure, when the time comes, Elijah will allow me to remain in residence."

"Don't be dramatic," her mother said and sighed. "You are far from becoming a spinster. Try being a little more…amiable. Allow yourself to like someone and see where it leads."

The problem with that was the only gentleman she found appealing didn't truly want her. When they crossed paths, they argued more often than not. She couldn't even begin to discern the best way to fix that between them. If they couldn't find any sort of harmony, they had no chance of any real future together.

She had given up on that notion a long time ago. Hyacinth had told him she hated him several times;

however, she had never truly felt that emotion for him. Though, admittedly, sometimes she didn't like him overly much, but that was when he was being especially mean. Most of the time, she secretly adored him. Her ambition to be a princess was her way of setting those feelings aside. If she couldn't have love, she might as well have an incredible title. "Mother, you found love and expect everyone can. Most individuals are not as lucky. Let me find my own way, and please stop with the unwelcome advice."

"There is no need to be rude," her mother huffed the words out.

"Don't worry, cousin," Scarlett said. "Love is already with you. Soon it will be undeniable."

Hyacinth wrinkled her nose. "I don't think I want to try to discern the meaning of that." She stared at Scarlett. "What of you? Do you have love in your life?"

She frowned. "My future is always unclear to me. The closer I am to something, the harder it is to see. I'd like to believe I will have love, but I can't be certain."

It hadn't occurred to Hyacinth that Scarlett's gift had a flaw. What good was it to have any visions of the future if she could not see her own? Hyacinth would hate it if she were in Scarlett's place. "I'm sure love will find you. How could it not?"

"Thank you." Scarlett's lips tilted upward into a warm smile. "I appreciate your belief in my happiness."

The carriage came to a stop in front of the manor. Hyacinth jerked forward a little as it halted. She held on to the side of the carriage to keep herself in place. "I'm glad we've finally arrive." She truly did hate traveling. It was one of the reasons she hadn't wanted to come to the house party. If she were to travel she'd have rather gone home instead.

"I couldn't agree more," Scarlett replied and blew out a breath. "There were times I thought we'd never arrive."

Hyacinth grinned. "Now you sound like Elijah." She couldn't help thinking about the last time she'd come to Weston. So much had happened on that visit. It had been the first long trip she'd taken with her mother and brother. It had also been when she'd first really noticed Lord Carrick. Maybe it would be cathartic to relive that time again. She could take a stroll through the caves and on the beach…exorcise him from her heart once and for all. "He complained the entire trip we made here a decade earlier."

Her mother chuckled. "He doesn't tolerate long

periods in a carriage well. That boy avoids them at all costs and now prefers to ride his horse." She shook her head. "It's probably for the best. There were times on that trip I considered murdering him, and I do love him."

"I am sure no one would have blamed you," Hyacinth told her. "He was insufferable." It was slightly amusing and heartening to hear her mother admit that Elijah had faults. It could be irritating to hear his accomplishments toted on a daily basis.

A footman opened the door to the carriage. He reached inside and assisted the ladies out. Hyacinth stretched relieved to finally be able to move freely. They had arrived. Now she had to implement her plan and see if she could live with Prince Adrian. She would like to think she could, but something inside her screamed that she'd hate every second of it. "Well, Mother," Hyacinth began, "I don't know about you and Scarlett, but I am looking forward to resting in my chambers. It's been quite the tedious journey to get here."

"I understand completely," her mother said. "Let's go greet the lady of the house, and then we can all rest."

Scarlett nodded. "You don't need to convince me. I'm ready and willing to sleep the rest of the day."

She rubbed her tummy. "Or at least until dinner. My stomach might disagree with sleeping through the night."

Hyacinth chuckled. They might irritate her every now and then, but they were her family, and she adored them. Once she was certain they were both settled into their rooms though, she fully intended to leave and explore the grounds. Hyacinth had plans, and they didn't include any sort of chaperone.

RHYS STARED AT THE BEACH BELOW THE CLIFFS. HE'D been at Weston less than an hour, and he'd already grown restless. Lady Hyacinth had arrived shortly after, but he'd made sure to escape before she noticed. After their last encounter, he'd had a lot to think about.

What did he want for his life? Was being a spy worth giving up everything else? Some days, he wasn't so sure that it would be. His father had been a spy for years before settling down and marring his mother. Rhys had thought he could do the same…be a spy and maybe settle down later in life. The difference between him and his father was the need for spies had diminished. There were no wars. At least, nothing major that everyone took notice of. There might be something down the road. One could never truly know what the future might hold. He could only hope that he made the right decision for himself, and what he believed he owed his country.

"Are you thinking of jumping?" Christian asked, his tone light with amusement.

Rhys jumped, startled at his approach. He'd been inside his head and had tuned out the world around him. "I hadn't considered it. Do you think I should?" he deadpanned.

Christian shrugged. "It might have its benefits."

"How so?" Rhys lifted a brow. The conversation had taken a slightly morbid tone; although, he didn't fully believe his cousin was serious. Still, his curiosity got the better of him, and he couldn't help playing along.

"Well, there is the obvious." Christian stared down. "Your misery would end when you go splat on the sand below."

Rhys rocked back on his heels and tilted his head to the side. "There is that." He glanced down and narrowed his gaze. "It would make this thing we call living essentially easier considering I would no longer be breathing. Any decisions I might need to make can continue unmade." He'd never jump to escape his problems. That's not the way to solve anything, and it would make the lives of those he left behind miserable. How did that solve anything? The answer was simple—it didn't.

"True," Christian said. "Then there is the other possibility. Though, from what I understand of it, I'm not sure you qualify."

"I'm not sure I follow," Rhys said. Christian could talk circles around anyone, and his head was currently spinning from that last sentence. "I may need you to explain."

"Did you know my mother fell off this cliff once," he began. "She's not the only one either. There was another woman who did as well. Though, to be fair, both fell from the future into the past. I'm not certain it would work in reverse."

Rhys shook his head baffled. "So, my other option is time travel. Though I might possibly go farther back instead of to the future."

Christian shrugged. "One can never tell. It's a risky proposition either way. I wouldn't recommend it. Nicholas took a safer path, but even that wasn't exactly a sound decision. He had no idea of knowing if it would work or not."

"I detect some bitterness," Rhys said. "Did he not discuss his decision with you?"

If Rhys had a brother, let alone a twin, it might bother him too if he decided to leave without a word. He adored his sister, Charlotte, and he'd be pissed at her for risking her safety on a lark. His heart beat heavily in his chest at the very thought of it. He wanted to rush inside and ensure that she remained safe in the salon with his Aunt Alys and his mother.

"He left a note," Christian said, "of sorts. If he was here, I'd throttle him."

"I'm sorry," he said softly. "I know how close you two were...are." Nicholas wasn't dead. He had decided to abandon his family for a grand adventure. Rhys didn't doubt he landed safely wherever he was. "I do hope he returns one day."

"He won't," Christian said. "Elizabeth had a vision of him in the mirror. He's in love."

"Ah..." Rhys sighed. Love seemed to drive them all. They were all prone to it. A family trait none of them could escape even if they wanted to. "At least you know he's all right."

"Yeah," Christian said, but his tone was dry. "I'll learn to accept it. I'm happy for him even if I'm incredibly pissed at the bloody arse."

Rhys smacked him on the back. "Have faith. One day you'll fall in love too, and you'll learn to be more forgiving of Nicholas's choice." In some ways, Rhys envied Nicholas. He'd decided what he wanted and risked everything to have it.

Christian remained quiet for several seconds. "Perhaps…" He blew out a breath. "So I can be reasonably assured you are not going to jump?"

Rhys shook his head. "That was never my intention. I love life too much to even consider it. Though I might take the cave path to go down the beach. A walk along the shore may be what I need most."

He honestly had no idea what he needed. Rhys couldn't stop thinking about Lady Hyacinth and if he desired her more than he wanted to work for the home office. So far, he was failing miserably at everything he'd been tasked to do. He watched the prince, but whenever Lady Hyacinth was near he paid more attention to her.

"All right," Christian said. He still had a touch of melancholy in his tone. "Then I'll leave you to it. Father has tasked me with visiting some of the tenants. Will you meet me later for a game of billiards?"

"Absolutely," he agreed. A game of billiards might be a good way to round off the evening. "It would be my pleasure."

Christian turned on his heels and left. Rhys

stared after him for a few moments and then headed to the cave entrance. He would head down to the beach and maybe go for a swim. He would be relatively undisturbed. No one but family would dare go to the caves and most of them were occupied elsewhere. A vigorous swim might be exactly what he needed to help him settle his thoughts. At the very least, it might exhaust him enough he could sleep later that night.

CHAPTER 7

Hyacinth sneaked away from the manor and headed toward the cliffs. The sun had started descending from the sky, and it was a little darker outside, but not enough to make it difficult to see. She didn't want to wait until nightfall. She remembered how dark the caves could be, and she wouldn't have Lord Carrick to help lead her through them. A part of her wished she could have him with her; the other part was grateful to be alone. She wanted it to be her and the ocean below. Something about watching the waves crash to shore helped her relax and think.

She reached the entrance to the path that led to the caves. It was steeper than she remembered, and she had to brace herself on the wall as she moved slowly down. With each step, she breathed a little easier. Her heart raced as she made her way down. It was a little thrilling to do this on her own. No one was around to judge her, and there was something freeing in that. Tomorrow, she would focus on the prince and decide if she wanted to convince him she'd make the perfect wife. Today she would devote solely to herself. She reached the end of the path and stepped out on to the beach. Hyacinth closed her eyes and took a deep breath. The scent of saltwater and sand greeted her.

The moon was full overhead, and as the sky darkened further, it allowed a little light for her. She moved closer to the beach. She wanted to wade in the water as it washed to shore. Should she take off her shoes, lift her skirt, and push her toes into the sand? The very idea thrilled her. She walked to a nearby boulder and sat down to remove her stockings and shoes. Once her feet were free, she pushed them into the sand and sighed. It was wonderful. Now all she needed was to walk along the shore and feel the waves as they rolled over her feet.

She stood and walked toward the shore. Once she neared, she lifted her skirts and waded a little into the water. Hyacinth was so glad she'd taken the time to come to the beach. This had to be the best decision she'd ever made. She could not recall a more perfect moment.

The echoes of splashing surrounded her. She turned toward the origin of the sounds and frowned. Was someone swimming in the ocean? Hyacinth narrowed her gaze and frowned. She couldn't quite make out the object in the water. It could be anything, but she feared it might be a person. It may or may not be one of the residents of Weston Manor. Whoever it was clearly had decided to try a little ocean bathing. Perhaps she should gather her belongings and leave before the person swimming noticed her. The figure swam closer and she could start to see more of them. She could be wrong, but she suspected it was a person, and a man. Hyacinth nibbled on her lips, transfixed. Her curiosity was about to get the best of her. She wanted to know the person's identity—man or woman. It would be a juicy tidbit she might be able to use to her advantage.

Lord Carrick stepped out of the water and started toward her. He had been the one swimming. He hadn't noticed her, and it was too late for her to scamper away. When he reached her, he glanced up and cursed. "Sweetness," he said, "what the blazes are you doing here?"

A lump formed in her throat as she took in everything. He had been swimming naked... His clothes were laying on the rock separating them. She hadn't noticed them before, and did now because she had to look somewhere other than directly at him, but she kept sneaking quick glances. If it wasn't dark, she probably would have been able to see every inch of his bare skin. The only thing preventing that in its entirety was the boulder he stood behind. It was high enough to stop above his manhood but left his upper body completely exposed.

Hyacinth gave up and stared boldly at him. If he wasn't worried about his nakedness, why should she? She should look away but refused to, and if she were to be honest with herself, she didn't want to. Lord Carrick was one gorgeous man. "It appears I'm here to witness your scandalous activity."

He rolled his eyes. "No one should have been able to witness anything. Go back up to the house."

"No." She had come to the beach for her own reasons. Hyacinth hadn't expected to see him, but now that she had... She would be a fool not to take advantage of the situation. Perhaps this is the reason she'd been drawn to the cliffs and the beach below.

"No?" He shook his head and mumbled something else she couldn't quite hear. "You are determined to make me miserable, aren't you?"

"Of course not," she huffed. "But I'm not about to allow you to dictate my actions. I'm going to walk on the beach as I intended. You do whatever you please. It means nothing to me."

He reached over and yanked his breaches off the boulder and shrugged them on. Too bad... She would have enjoyed a better glance at his attributes. What she had seen was spectacular. Hyacinth sighed. The trek down the beach had been worth the effort. She strolled along the shore and soaked her feet in the salty spray. Hyacinth kept her skirts lifted so she didn't get the hem soaked.

"You're not acting very ladylike," he shouted to her. "Ladies don't lift their skirts in the presence of a man."

She snorted. "No one will know, and you don't even like me. I doubt the sight of my ankles is going to suddenly make you overcome with desire."

"You never know," he leaned down to whisper those words huskily in her ear. She nearly jumped at his unexpected closeness. "I might indeed find you incredibly desirable. That sneak peek of more tantalizing, creamy skin might make me overcome with lust."

"Don't be ridiculous," she retorted. He couldn't be serious. But if he was…did she want to push the issue? Hyacinth had the urge to lean back into him and press her body against his. He hadn't bothered to fully dress. Even though he'd swam in the ocean, heat still poured off his body and enveloped her. Her words were breathy as she spoke, "Don't pretend to feel something you do not. It's not very becoming."

"But you are, sweetness," his voice was husky. He trailed his fingers down her bare arm, and she shivered from his touch. "You're breathtaking."

Hyacinth closed her eyes and lost herself in the moment, his touch, and the silky smoothness of his voice. She'd dreamed of this. What it would be like to be the sole focus of this man. How could she ever consider marrying another when she wanted Lord Carrick? She loved him. Had always loved him. The only reason she snarled at him was because he'd always been indifferent to her. The only sign he might like her more than he showed was his nickname for her: *sweetness*. She never heard him refer to anyone else with that moniker. Could she be brave enough to take a chance with him? Hyacinth wasn't certain she could be that vulnerable. "Didn't I tell you not to pretend to like me?" She hated how much it hurt to say those words.

"I never said I didn't like you," he told her.

"You didn't have to," her voice wobbled a little as she spoke. Her emotions poured out into her words. "Your actions say everything I needed to hear."

"Not everything," he insisted. He lifted his hand and brushed back her hair, leaving her face free from the flyaway strands. "There is so much I have never said in word or deed."

Hyacinth wanted to believe him. She didn't know if she could, but oh, did she want to. She wanted to beg him to love her, to need her, the way she did him. It might prove to be her undoing if she did though. There was a very real chance it could be the biggest mistake of her life too. There was so much risk. The reward would be considerable though… "What are you trying to say now?" She leaned against him. Hyacinth could no longer resist the urge.

"Hell if I know," he admitted. "I may have lost my mind." He pressed his lips against her jaw. "You make me crazy."

"I don't mean to." He drove her to the brink of insanity too. What did that say about them?

"I believe you." He wrapped one of his arms around her waist. She was grateful for it because her legs had started to wobble. His cheek was flush with hers. Her entire body had warmed so much she wanted to strip her dress off and soak in the ocean to cool herself. He trailed his fingers across her waist. "I think we were created for each other, and denying that is what makes us do and say things we don't mean."

That made some strange sort of sense to her. "Maybe…"

She should push him away. This was all wrong, and if they were caught… Hyacinth didn't want a forced marriage. She may have strong feelings for him, but she had no way of discerning what he felt for her. There was desire. That part she could no longer deny. It was evident in his touch and the way her body was on the brink of bursting into flames. The fire inside of her had risen to an unbearable degree.

"Do you doubt it?"

"There is little room to question the veracity of your deduction. We both feel this…whatever this is between us. That doesn't mean we should give in to it." She wanted to scream…she needed him so much. "This is not right."

"It's very right," he disagreed with her. "Nothing has ever felt more right than this. I'm done fighting it."

"No," she said. Hyacinth wanted him so much. If she gave in to this need, with him, then she'd have to give up on her ambitions. Hyacinth would never be a princess, and she had doubts he wanted anything permanent with her. She would not fall victim to her own libido—even if she had real feelings for him. She couldn't do this though. "I can't."

She pulled away from him and stumbled over to the boulder where she had left her shoes and stockings. Tears threatened to fall. She had come down to the beach to explore what she wanted. Of course Lord Carrick would be there. He had been in the forefront of her mind for weeks now. He was offering himself to her, but for how long? An hour? A night? She hadn't heard anything to suggest he wanted forever with her. Hyacinth would not allow herself to fall into something meaningless. Desire could destroy her and her ambition. Love could be her everything, but she heard no flowery words or promises from him. She deserved more than a few stolen moments.

"Sweetness…" He had grabbed his shirt and slid it on. He was still barefoot and wild as the sea though. "Please don't go."

"Stop," she said. "I've made up my mind." It hurt but she had to be true to herself. Loving him might ruin her. *Had* ruined her if she were to be honest with herself. She doubted she could ever feel anything as strong for another man. "It's best we didn't take things far. It would have been a mistake."

"It isn't a mistake," he growled out the words. He stalked forward and pulled her into his arms. "This is not something so easily forgotten." He leaned down and pressed his lips to hers. The fire reignited and burst into something more monumental than she could have imagined. The press of his lips on hers, the taste of his tongue as it entwined with hers, and the scent of salt on his skin all added to the meaningful moment. Hyacinth had never been kissed like this. It shattered her heart and made her weep with joy, but no tears actually fell from her eyes. She loved him. Always would. The kiss changed nothing.

It took every ounce of strength she had, but she pulled away. She would never forget this kiss. Hyacinth didn't want to. It would be something to keep her warm at night when nothing but cold surrounded her. This was the kiss she'd always dreamed she could have, but never believed she'd get. It was perfect. He was almost perfect.

But he wasn't meant to be hers.

"Thank you," she said and turned away from him.

"Where are you going, sweetness?" Concern mixed with frustration was etched through his voice as he spoke.

Her heart froze in her chest. "Don't call me that anymore."

"I'm incapable of doing that. You're everything sweet, and you're mine."

She glanced over her shoulder and said firmly, "I belong to myself. No one owns me."

"Please…" He almost sounded desperate, but she would not let that sway her. Even if it broke her heart a little to walk away from him.

Hyacinth shook her head firmly. "Lord Carrick…"

"Rhys," he said. "I think we can dispense with formalities. Say my name, sweetness."

She said it inside her head…*Rhys*… Hyacinth would not say it aloud. It would give him too much power. Though she did like the sound of it. In another lifetime, she would have loved to have the right to say it whenever she chose. "Lord Carrick," she began again. "I am returning to the manor. Please, I implore you, wait a while before you return as well. Have care with my reputation." With those words, she left him alone. She had a lot to think about.

CHAPTER 8

Rhys stared out the window of the game room. The billiards match with Christian had gone by in a blur, and he was confident he'd lost, but as he barely paid attention, it didn't surprise him. He was normally quite competitive; however, his thoughts remained fixed on his encounter with Lady Hyacinth on the beach. He couldn't shake it and honestly wasn't certain he wanted to.

"Are you all right?" Christian asked.

"Yes," he answered instinctively. "Why would you believe otherwise?" Rhys didn't want to admit that he was far from being all right. He'd never felt more unsettled in his entire life. Nothing seemed definite to him, and he had no idea what to do about it.

Christian lifted a brow. "Has it escaped your notice how deplorable you played?"

"I don't know what you are suggesting," he said without a twitch of his lip to give him away. "Do you believe I lost on purpose? To what end?"

"That's not what I said at all." Christian sighed. "You never play poorly. In fact, you are quite difficult to beat at any game, so there must be something ailing you for you to have lost this badly. What the blazes is wrong with you?"

"Not a thing," Rhys answered. *Only everything...* "I'm a bit preoccupied is all." What was Lady Hyacinth doing at this moment? Should he search for her? Would she give him the cut direct? God help him, he was turning into a maudlin fool. If he kept up this line of thought, he might lose the right to his own masculinity. He had to do something, anything, to help distract him from his thoughts of Lady Hyacinth. "Where's the brandy?" He needed a drink, or several.

"Hello, gentlemen," Prince Adrian said as he entered the game room. "Did I hear someone mention brandy? I could use a snifter myself."

Rhys held back a sneer. There was something about the prince that he abhorred. His demeanor left little to be desired, and he was off-putting at best. He would not snub the prince though. Rhys would do his duty even if it sat heavily inside of him. He walked over to the bar and poured three glasses, then handed one to Christian and Prince Adrian. "Glad to oblige," he said, then picked up his own glass. He saluted the prince. "Cheers." Rhys took a hefty drink. It burned as it traveled down his throat, but he barely felt it. He couldn't help thinking he should be careful what he wished for. Mere moments ago, he'd been wishing for something to distract him, and here the prince was to do that.

"Thank you," Prince Adrian said. "Are you playing billiards?"

"We finished our game," Christian said, then took a drink of his own brandy. "Are you hoping for a match?"

"Perhaps," the prince replied. "It's been a while since I've had a decent opponent. How well do you fare at the game?"

"I play passably," Christian told him. "I don't play nearly as well as my cousin." He patted Rhys on the shoulder. "Though, for some reason tonight, he's not at his best."

The hell he wasn't. He could beat the prince, and he would. "Now, now, don't go making the prince think I'm subpar," Rhys said. "I'm certain I can muster up some basic skills if the prince wishes to play."

Prince Adrian's lips turned up into a cocky smile. Rhys wanted to wipe it away with his fist but held back the urge. "I'd be happy to play a little game with Lord Carrick if he would be willing to indulge me."

"Far be it from me to prevent it," Christian said. "I'll be a happy spectator." He sipped more of his brandy. "By and by, where is that manservant of yours that is always following you around. What's his name again?"

"You mean Marius?" Prince Adrian grabbed one of the billiard sticks as Rhys set up the table. "He's taking care of an errand for me. I don't need him with me for everything. I'm more than capable to seeing to my needs."

Rhys couldn't believe the man had admitted that, at times, he was incapable of taking care of himself. What a dandy. Surely he hadn't been truthful with that statement. He had to understand how that made him look. "You may go first," he told the prince. Rhys wanted to gauge how the man played.

The prince went to the table and lined up his shot. He scored a few points before he made an error, leaving the table to Rhys. He had been distracted while playing Christian. With the prince, his focus was on the table, and the prince. "How is your visit thus far?" he asked. He lined up his shot and hit the ball. He scored and went to line up another shot.

"It's been wonderful," the prince admitted. "Everyone has been so welcoming. I especially have enjoyed Lady Hyacinth's company."

Rhys almost missed the shot and would have been behind. Luckily, he compensated quickly, and while he didn't gain the points he hoped, it was still his turn. "She's quite lovely," he begrudgingly admitted.

"I think so too," Prince Adrian said. "She'd make a lovely princess."

His stomach sank at his words. Rhys squeezed the billiard stick and barely refrained from snapping it in half. Would Lady Hyacinth agree to marry this dandy? She deserved so much more than *him*. The title would probably appeal to her though. How could it not? He could make her a princess. What could Rhys offer her?

Love. He could offer her love. His title might not be as grand, but he would cherish her forever. All he had to do was convince her of that. The prince could go to hell. "Are you going to offer for her?" He had to ask, had to know, what he was up against.

"I may," the prince said. "I haven't made a decision yet. I have to...how do you say it? ...Test the lady's willingness."

Did he mean... "Are you going to seduce her?" He'd murder the bloody bastard.

"Of course not," the prince said, then winked. "A gentleman would never do such a thing."

Rhys hit the ball and ended the game as fast as it started. He was done. He couldn't spend another second in Prince Adrian's company. If he did, he would strangle him, and then he'd end up in prison for killing a foreign royal prince. "If you'll pardon me, I'm suddenly exhausted. It was a pleasure to play billiards with you." Rhys bowed and rushed from the room, his fists clenched the entire time he exited.

THE SUN'S RAYS FELL ACROSS HIS FACE AND BLINDED him. His head throbbed as tiny hammers pounded all around his skull. Rhys had found some brandy and took it to his bedchamber where he drank the entire bottle before passing out in bed. His eyes were raw and gritty, and he had to look like hell. He certainly felt like it. What had he been thinking? He hadn't been, or he'd never have imbibed so much.

That bloody arse was going to try to seduce Lady Hyacinth.

Rhys would not let that happen. He had to get his act together and do something to save her. She might not appreciate it in the moment, but in time she'd forgive him. He was only looking out for her and her virtue. Hadn't she asked him to have a care for her reputation? Well, damn it, he was going to do that whether she liked it or not.

It had nothing to do with the fact he loved her and wanted her for himself. No. Nothing at all. Now that he had that settled, he best get himself presentable. It was going to be a long day. He couldn't be certain when the prince planned to pounce, so he had to be ready for anything. God, his head hurt…

He went over to the washbasin and did his best to wash the brandy inducing disgust from his face. His head still hurt, but his eyes felt a little less like they had been seared shut. Feeling a little better, he slowly dressed. Why had he told his valet to stay in London? He had lost his mind. Clearly, this deficit had started before Rhys had come to Weston Manor. Lady Hyacinth had turned him into a bloody imbecile.

Rhys dressed. It was slow and painful, but

somehow he managed. Then he stumbled out of his room and down the stairs. He made it down them without breaking his neck. He considered that a huge success. So far, so good.

The breakfast room was nearly empty. The only person at the table was…Lady Hyacinth. She wore a soft pink day dress with a matching spencer. It made her even lovelier. He adored her in pink, but she probably hated the color. It was almost too timid for her fiery spirit. What were the odds? At least that dandy hadn't been there too. He'd barely managed to not kill him the night before. Rhys was certain doing so at breakfast would not have gone over well. "Good morning," he said.

"Is it?" Lady Hyacinth lifted a brow. "It's raining. We're to be stuck inside the entire day."

Rhys wasn't sure if that was good or not. It might be easier to watch the prince and ascertain his actions if they were confined to the house. Lady Hyacinth was prone to wandering around the estate too. Yes, he liked the idea of the house being the only place they could go. "Doesn't seem too horrible," he told her. "Isn't the ball tonight anyway?"

She wrinkled her nose. "How can you not find this horrid? Everyone will have to travel in the rain. All the dresses will get wet and muddy…"

"How is that your concern?" He was genuinely confused. "You don't *have* to leave the house."

"I suppose that is true." She sighed. The level of disappointment in her voice was enough to make his heart ache. "I hate the rain. It's so dreary." He'd will the rain away if it were in his power. Sadly, he didn't have the ability to control the weather. He hated seeing her so miserable.

All it was doing for him was making him sleepy. Rhys wanted to turn around and go back to his room and rest…for hours, maybe days. He stared at her, struck with the idea that he could lock her in the room with him, and then he could sleep while keeping her safe. No. That was a terrible idea. He'd never be able to sleep. She would either scream bloody murder or he'd be the one seducing her, maybe both.

"What is wrong with you?" she asked.

Why did everyone keep asking him that? To be fair, only Christian and Lady Hyacinth had bothered to ask. "I'm fine. Why do you ask?"

She tilted her head to the side. "You seem…" She nibbled on her lip, and he was momentarily transfixed. "You're not yourself. Do you feel well?" She moved her hand to place it on his head, and he almost jerked away on reflex, but stood still. "You don't feel warm. Still…" She studied him. "You look ill."

"It's nothing." His voice was hoarse. "It's kind of you to be concerned, but there's no need to worry."

She shrugged. "I'd hate for you to miss the ball. It's to be the only real entertainment we have. I am excited. The prince is going to dance with me."

His stomach soured. He wouldn't be able to eat anything of substance. Rhys went to the breakfast board and put some toast on his plate. He would eat some dry toast and tea. If he was lucky, he'd be able to keep both down. "You shouldn't dance with him."

"Why not?" she asked. Her tone sounded defensive.

"He doesn't have good intentions toward you," he told her. Maybe if he had been honest with her, she'd actually listen.

"Don't be ridiculous." Lady Hyacinth rolled her eyes. "He's been nothing but a gentleman."

He stared at her. How could he make her understand the danger she was putting herself in. "He's not a good man." He kept his words quiet and firm. Maybe if he stayed somber, she'd see the truth.

"I don't have to listen to this." She frowned. "You're being mean. I don't know why, but I don't like it. Keep your thoughts to yourself."

He reached for her, but he was too late. She was past him and out of the breakfast room before he could stop her. Rhys sighed. He'd have to get himself together and keep watch over her. He wouldn't allow her to be hurt in any fashion.

CHAPTER 9

Hyacinth strolled into the ballroom. She may not be a princess, but she certainly felt like one. Her dress was perfect in every way, and it wasn't a pale color. The gown had been made with red velvet and ruffled white silk, and it was all hers. She had a seamstress make it for her in secret, and she'd saved it for a special moment. One she would use in rebellion against society's, her mother's, and everyone's expectations and rules for her. Hyacinth couldn't be the good girl any longer. She wanted to prove something to herself and the world.

She could make decisions for herself. No one had the right to tell her who she could be or would be. This was her time to shine. Her one moment to be who she always dreamed she could be, and the *ton* could be damned.

After this ball, she would return to Havenwood and live a quiet life. Hyacinth no longer wished to be a princess. She needed one thing: freedom. She wanted to make her own decisions and live her life as she chose. Today marked the beginning of doing exactly as she pleased, when she so desired, whatever and whenever she decided to. The dress was that bold statement, and she couldn't wait for the *ton* to take notice.

Hyacinth lifted her lips into a wanton smile. The sheer joy flowing through her was indescribable. Why had she not taken control of her life sooner? She didn't need to marry to find happiness. She found it within herself. Lord Carrick…Rhys…hadn't needed to warn her about the prince. She would dance with Prince Adrian and then leave him in her past. It mattered not what his intentions were in regard to her. She didn't want him and would not marry him even if he begged.

"Lady Hyacinth," the prince greeted her and bowed. "May I say how lovely you look tonight?"

"You may," she said. She'd never felt more beautiful. Even her hair had been adorned in an elaborate chignon with tiny seed pearls pinned throughout her dark locks. She grinned cheekily. "I trust you find this ball to your liking."

"It is now," he answered. "You've finally arrived. May I sign your dance card?"

She lifted it for him and he scrawled his name on the first dance. A quadrille…she was grateful for his choice. She didn't want an intimate dance like the waltz with Prince Adrian. If given the choice, she'd leave those all open to Lord Carrick. She wanted to refer to him as Rhys as he'd asked, but she feared if she started in her mind, she'd slip and say it aloud. That would make them seem a familiarity between them that didn't exist. Though admittedly it had gone pretty far between them on the beach. "I look forward to our dance," she told Prince Adrian. "Pardon me. I must find my mother."

Hyacinth turned and left the prince to his many admirers. One time she would have counted herself amongst the many who wanted to gain his attention. Now that she had, it seemed almost…silly. Why had she thought her worth should be measured by a man and his title? If she ever married, and she doubted she would, it would be for love as her parents had. Having a better title and station than someone she deemed a rival of sorts was an absurd goal. Hyacinth was glad she'd given up on having one.

She bumped into a lady as she strolled around the ballroom absentmindedly. "My apologies, I should have paid better attention."

The woman had blonde hair with a mix of gold and white streaked through it. She had delicate features and stunning blue eyes. The same shade as Lord Carrick's... It had to be a coincidence. She smiled brazenly at her and then said in a bright tone, "I'm sure I'm as much at fault. It's my first ball, and I'm so excited I've bounced around more than I should."

"Your first ball," Hyacinth replied. "How wonderful for you."

"It's a country ball, so my mother thought I was finally old enough to attend, and well, its family."

She was related to the Duke of Weston? She did look similar to the Duchess and Lady Elizabeth. All that blonde hair... The only way to gain her name would to be to provide her own. "I'm Lady Hyacinth Barrington," she introduced herself.

"Lady Charlotte Rossington," the young girl said. She couldn't be more than seventeen, maybe eighteen if Hyacinth was any good at guessing. She was also Lord Carrick's little sister.

"Have you found a dance partner yet?" Hyacinth

asked. "She nodded. "Though I doubt my brother counts. He's dancing the quadrille with me."

A chaste dance for a brother to dance with his sister…Hyacinth approved. "How kind of him. My brother couldn't be bothered to attend the ball. He has better things to do, I suppose."

Lady Charlotte wrinkled her nose. "All men believe that their tasks are more important than balls, and most of them think they are far more intelligent. Aunt Alys said its best to allow them the luxury of believing that and then steer them secretly in the direction you wish them to go. Sometimes cleverness is best left hidden."

"I think I like your Aunt Alys." Who she suspected was the Duchess of Weston. "She sounds like quite the smart lady."

"Oh, she is," Lady Charlotte agreed. "A lady out of time, some might say."

Hyacinth tilted her head to the side. What did she mean by that? "I wouldn't know," she said. She wasn't even going to try to guess as to what Lady Charlotte referred to. It hurt her head to even think about it.

"Trust me," she said. "Aunt Alys is special." She grinned and then waved across the room at someone. "There's Rhys now."

He was near. Why did he have to affect her this way? Why did she desire him? It would have been so much easier if she'd wanted the prince. He seemed to desire her...

Lady Charlotte did the unladylike action of hugging her brother tightly in public. It was nice to see two siblings who appeared to adore each other. Hyacinth was a little jealous of that.

"Lady Hyacinth," he greeted her with a nod.

"Lord Carrick," she repeated the gesture.

"Oh, you two know each other?" Lady Charlotte beamed at them both. "You should sign her dance card, Rhys. There is only one name on it."

"Oh, he doesn't..."She fought a blush that threatened to stain her cheeks. Hyacinth had never felt so embarrassed in her life, but if she kept protesting it would only make it worse.

"Don't listen to her," Lady Charlotte interrupted. "I noticed even though she tried to hide it." Had she? Hyacinth didn't think she had, but maybe Lady Charlotte believed it. "She's too pretty to be left without dance partners. Isn't she lovely?"

Rhys glanced at her and held her gaze. His eyelids drooped a little low, almost seductively, and it sent tiny shivers down her spine. Her heart beat so hard it seemed it might burst from her chest. She gave up referring to him as Lord Carrick in that moment. Her heart was his and always had been. She'd wanted to hate him. Had even stated she did aloud on several occasions, but she didn't. Never had…

"She is indeed quite lovely," he said a little huskily. "I'd be happy to dance with her."

Without giving her a chance to object, he lifted the card and wrote his name on it, not bothering to actually look at the card or the name of the gentleman who'd already signed it. For some reason, she was grateful he hadn't perused it too much. She didn't look at it either. Somehow, she knew exactly what dance he'd claimed. The second dance, the one after the quadrille, the waltz… The one she had hoped he'd take but never thought he would. She wanted to hug Charlotte for the gift she'd given her. "If you'll pardon me, I see my cousin Scarlett." She turned to Lady Charlotte. "I hope to see you again later. Enjoy your first ball."

With those words, she turned on her heels and crossed the ballroom. She needed some distance between her and Rhys. The dance would bring them closer together, and she wasn't certain if she'd be able to keep how she felt hidden. She needed time to settle what her heart held inside of it and prayed she'd keep that love a secret for a little while longer. She wanted to enjoy the dance, not fear its outcome.

RHYS STARED AT HYACINTH'S RETREATING FORM. HE couldn't help thinking of her as only *Hyacinth*. His heart wouldn't allow any more formality to stand between them, even in his thoughts. His sister had done him a great favor by suggesting he sign Hyacinth's dance card. He owed her, and he'd repay Charlotte later. He still had to get through the quadrille before he could claim Hyacinth for their dance. It felt as if it would take forever for that inevitable outcome. He wanted to hold her, claim her, and make her, *his*, in every way. First, he had to convince her he was worth taking a risk on. She didn't seem to believe he was worthy of her. Truthfully, he didn't blame her for that deduction. He wasn't. No one could ever be perfect for her; however, he wanted to dedicate his life to making her every wish come true. Surely that was an endeavor that might at the very least soften her heart to him.

He loved her.

Rhys liked to think she felt the same way about

him. He'd move heaven and Earth if possible to prove to her that he adored her. Worshiped her... Needed her more than he could ever put into words. For now though, he would have to give his sister his full attention. This was her first ball, and she had to be brimming with excitement.

The band gathered on a nearby staging area to play. Rhys turned to his sister and held out his hand, "I believe this is my dance."

She giggled. "Indeed it is, my lord." Charlotte placed her hand in his, and he led her to the floor. They all lined up across from each other to prepare for the quadrille. It didn't escape his notice that Hyacinth had walked on to the floor with Prince Adrian. The muscles in his cheek clenched. There was nothing to do about it. Rhys would dance with her after this one and attempt to get her alone afterward. Then he could try again to convince her that the prince had bad intentions toward her.

The quadrille went by in a blur. At one juncture, he had Hyacinth in front of him, but he didn't meet her gaze. He was afraid he'd react poorly. Rhys had to maintain his composure. He could be patient even if it killed him. Finally, the dance ended and he could seek out Hyacinth for their waltz.

The moments between dances were grueling.

Sweat beaded on his forehead, but it wasn't from the humid weather. This was all about his anxiety and the forthcoming dance. He searched the room and finally located Hyacinth on the far end. She was in a deep discussion with his cousin, Elizabeth. He furrowed his eyebrows, confused at the sight. He didn't think Hyacinth and Elizabeth liked each other… Perhaps he should join them and hopefully keep the peace. If he planned on having Hyacinth in his life, he'd prefer they at least tolerated each other.

Rhys moved toward them in long, fast strides. He dodged and weaved through the guests with precision he hadn't been aware he had been capable of. When he reached them, he'd been expecting them to be sharing barbs, but they were…laughing. It puzzled him, but at least he didn't have to separate them.

"Elizabeth," he greeted his cousin. "How are you? Where is Jack?" Her husband, the Duke of Whitewood, didn't like to be separated from her, and it was odd he wasn't by her side.

"He is in the card room. My father insisted, and Jack hates to disappoint him." Elizabeth grinned. "It is amusing to observe."

"I'm glad they are finding common interests." Rhys honestly didn't care. It was more a statement he thought sounded good than anything else. "I'm sure Uncle James is ensuring Jack hasn't become complacent. He wouldn't want him to neglect his duties to you."

"There is little chance Jack will ever do that. A man in love wants to please the object of his devotion." Rhys couldn't agree more. "How are you?" She smiled softly. "I have not had the chance to speak with you since I arrived." Hyacinth had been blessedly serene while Elizabeth talked. Rhys was losing whatever patience he had. "I'm fine." The musicians started to take their place again. "But you must pardon me. I've promised the next dance to Lady Hyacinth, and I believe it is about to begin."

"Have you now?" Elizabeth lifted a questioning brow. "Then by all means lead her to the floor." She gestured for Hyacinth to join him. She placed her hand in his, and he led her to the floor.

Once there, he swung her around, left one hand clasped with hers, and placed the other on her waist. They hadn't spoken a word, and it made him anxious. He usually did all right in silence, but he hated she was so quiet. The music began, and they started to move. She was graceful and followed his lead expertly.

"I feel I must apologize," Rhys began. "I handled our conversation this morning poorly."

"You didn't look in the best health," she supplied. "Perhaps it clouded your judgment."

He should have the grace to agree with her, but he couldn't. If he didn't make her understand the prince was a danger to her… He swallowed hard. He didn't want to consider the irreparable damage to her reputation and how it might diminish her life's goals. "Indeed," he agreed. "I did not feel well. Too much brandy often does that to a man." He smiled, but he didn't feel it. "But I don't regret trying to warn you. Only the way I approached you with it."

She pursed her lips in displeasure. "You are not going to attempt to dissuade me from any association with Prince Adrian again, are you?" She tilted her head to the side and wouldn't meet his gaze. "He was a perfect gentleman when we danced. There is no reason to assume he means me any harm."

"I'm not making any suppositions," he said decisively. "I would never do that. I work in facts. It is the reason I am so good at what I do." He stared down at her as he twirled her around the dance floor. "There are times that I work on instinct because that is all I have to go on, and while everything inside me screams Prince Adrian is the worst sort of man, that is not all I'm using to make my assessment." She finally met and held his gaze. "Trust me. He means to use you, and if he does, it will ruin you."

The dance came to an end, and he deposited her at the edge of the dance floor. He hoped he had managed to make her understand. There hadn't been nearly enough time. She lifted her chin defiantly. "Thank you for the dance, my lord. While I do believe you mean well, I am still unconvinced that your evaluation is the correct one. If you'll excuse me, I must visit the Lady's retiring room." With those words, she turned on her heel and rushed away from him. He cursed and started after her, but there were too many people, and he lost her in the crowd. Still, he had to find her, and he was determined to locate her straightaway. If she made it to the retiring room before he reached her, he'd have to wait for her to exit. He wanted to avoid that if he could. It wouldn't look good to be lurking outside. The ladies would think him a bigger scoundrel than some already did...

HYACINTH BLEW OUT A BREATH AND HEADED TOWARD

the library. There was unlikely to be any guests there, and she needed a few moments to herself. It didn't take her long to reach her destination. She stopped abruptly when voices echoed back at her. The door was ajar, and she could hear them clearly. She peeked inside. The prince and his manservant were in the room. They were standing relatively close to each other as they spoke, and had very serious expressions on their faces. Something must be wrong. Why else would they be huddled together during the middle of a ball?

"Are you certain she has a substantial dowry?" Prince Adrian asked.

"All my sources suggest she'll be well provided for. She's daddy's little girl, and he wants to ensure his precious daughter will is taken care of." Marius Alba was the other man with the prince. Hyacinth had little interaction with him, but he had always seemed...smarmy to her.

"Excellent," the prince replied. "There is only one thing left to do. I must ensure her agreement to the match. I cannot trust she'll agree on her own."

What lady was he hoping to make a match with, and why wouldn't she want to marry him? He had been talking to a lot of young misses, including her. Surely he wasn't referring to...her.

"Are you certain this is the route you wish to take," Mr. Alba asked. "She might hate you if you seduce her and force her hand in marriage."

How...deplorable. Her heart fell and her stomach churned. Did he really want to make her marry him? Would he also force himself on her? Mr. Alba said seduction, and that could be his fancy way of saying something more horrid. What reason would he have for doing something so...wrong? She hated to admit Rhys had been right, and she hoped he wouldn't taunt her with it.

"I have no choice," the prince said. "Our country is destitute. If I don't marry well, we will not survive. She can hate me all she wants, but in the end, she'll be a princess. Her sort likes the idea of a title. She'll acclimate because she won't have a choice. It's best she accepts that fact, and we will all be better off."

"You're right," Mr. Alba said, and then sighed. "What would you like me to do?"

"Deliver this missive to Lady Hyacinth and ensure she meets me here. I want to have some privacy with her so there is no doubt she agreed to be mine." He paused a moment and then continued, "Oh, and Marius, after a reasonable amount of time come back with a guest or two to discover us. Won't do any good if she's not thoroughly compromised."

Hyacinth gasped, and they turned toward the door. She tried to move out of view, but she feared they had seen her. There was only a small sliver open in the door. Perhaps she'd gone unnoticed. Her fears were founded when the door swung open and both men rushed toward her. She turned to flee and tripped over her skirt. It was too late. Prince Adrian clasped his hand over her wrist and yanked her into the library before she had any chance to get away. "It's unfortunate you had to hear that, but it changes nothing. This works for me too."

"It doesn't for me," she spat out the words.

The prince pulled her flush against him. It made her skin crawl, and she struggled against him. Why had she dismissed Rhys's warning? She should have listened, but she thought she knew better. A tear formed at the corner of her eye. She would have brushed it away, but Prince Adrian had both of her wrists secured in his hands now. He turned to the manservant and said, "Go have the carriage brought around. We are leaving with my bride-to-be immediately."

"Do you require my assistance with her?" Marius asked.

"No," the prince answered. "I think I can handle her on my own." With those words, the manservant spun on his heels and exited the library. Prince Adrian turned toward Hyacinth and pressed his lips to her cheek with a wet kiss before he spoke, "I must thank you for making this easier for me." He leaned down to kiss her, but she turned her head and his lips met her cheek. "I don't have to make this easy for you. I will have you, and you will like it. You're more of a spitfire than I gave you credit for."

The tear fell, and it was joined by more until her cheeks were completely wet. She wanted Rhys. Hyacinth would beg his forgiveness and tell him she loved him. She had so many regrets, and she feared she'd never have the chance to make up for those horrid choices.

"I hate you." She'd said those words to Rhys and never meant them. She did now. The prince was a horrible man. She couldn't believe she had ever considered marrying him.

"I'm all right with that." He pulled at her skirts. "That will make our couplings more interesting."

She froze at his words. He was really going to… She couldn't even think the word. It was all—surreal to her.

"Let her go," a man said in a hard voice. "If you hurt her I'll have to kill you, and I would hate to have to explain that to your consulate."

"Lord Carrick," the prince said in greeting. He had the audacity to sound contrite. "She's a lovely chit. You agreed with me last night during billiards."

"Because she's beautiful," Rhys said. "It's hard to disagree with the truth." He moved toward them with a grace and agility Hyacinth hadn't been aware he possessed. "But that does not give you the right to attack her and force yourself on her person. Now, do I need to repeat myself?"

"She is more than willing to receive my attentions." The prince still held her wrists. "I don't see any reason you would object to the lady choosing to share her virtue with me."

"I do mind," he said. "Because she's mine, and as I said, I really do not wish to murder you." Her heart had skipped a beat at his words. Had he claimed her as if he had a right to? Why did she like the idea of him taking control? She should be telling him he had no right because she belonged to no one, but she wanted to be his.

The prince stared at him with a shocked expression. "You're lying. My manservant checked, and she's unattached. She's more than able to affiance herself to me, and I am more than happy to start our...happiness before the wedding."

"I'm not marrying you," Hyacinth seethed. "And I

do not want you to touch me. Let me go." Somehow, she'd found her voice, and she had so many questions. Why was Rhys trying to say they were engaged though? What did he think he would gain by such a thing? The prince's actions had nearly undone her; however, Rhys had made her…hope. Did he love her?

"Lady Hyacinth is *mine*," he repeated and met her gaze. The determination in his voice and his expression told her so much, but not nearly enough. She still had questions, and later, when they were alone, she would have answers to them. "We've been secretly betrothed for months." He was lying, but she wouldn't contradict him. "She wanted to enjoy the rest of her season, and I was indulgent, but this ends now. Let my future wife go." He lifted a pistol she hadn't been aware he'd had and aimed it at the prince. "I won't tell you again."

The prince released her, and she fell to the floor with a loud *thud*, and pain shot through her backside. "You can have her. She's not worth this much effort. I have other ladies to choose from."

"Fair warning," Rhys began, "I sent word to the home office, and if you force yourself on any other unwilling ladies, you will not be welcome in this country and no English lady will be leaving with you. Go to another country in search of the heiress you need to refill your coffers. The ladies of England are not eligible to you. Our monarch will not approve the match."

The prince lifted his head high. "I don't want any of your insipid ladies anyway." With those words the prince stomped out of the room. Only after Rhys was certain he had gone did he lower the pistol. He calmly set it on a nearby table, rushed to her side and then brushed a few stray locks away. "Are you all right?" His hand shook as he caressed her. "Did he hurt you? I'll go after him and shoot him for daring to touch you."

She chuckled, but only because she could. He'd saved her. After she'd dismissed his warning as nothing, he still came to her rescue. Hyacinth lifted her head until her face was mere inches from his face. "I love you," she whispered and then pressed her lips to his. Heat flooded her as he took over the kiss. His tongue swept over hers with an expertise she didn't want to question.

He lifted his head. "I love you, too."

"Make love to me."

He lifted his head, taken aback. "I didn't admit how I felt so you'd agree to that."

"I know," she said. "But I refuse to deny myself

anything. I want you. I adore you, and I want to be with you in every way possible." She pressed her lips to his quickly. "Besides, we've been secretly engaged for months. Why not anticipate that wedding of ours and enjoy each other?"

"Hy…" He swallowed hard. "I do want to marry you. I should have asked, and I would have…"

"Yes," she said. "I'll marry you. Now please, make love to me. I need to wipe away the feel of his hands on me. Only you can do that."

Rhys slid his hand up her skirt and pressed a thumb to her center. He rubbed the tiny bud of nerves as he trailed kisses over her cheek and down to her neck. "As long as you understand that once we do this there is no going back. There will be a wedding."

"Anyone ever tell you that you talk too much?"

He chuckled lightly, and then there was no more need for words. They shed their clothes, and when they were both bare, he kneeled and spread her legs before him, then leaned down and kissed her inner thighs until he reached her sex. When he slid his tongue over her core, she nearly jumped, but he held her still. He kept kissing, licking and stroking her sex until she came undone and groaned with pleasure.

He kissed her again, this time on her belly. "That's it, sweetness," he coaxed. "Let go. I promise you'll enjoy it."

She'd never felt anything like it. This pleasure was almost unbearable. He moved over her and pressed himself against her center. His member was hard and seemed too big.

"I don't think we can do this…"

"We can," he told her, "but if you want me to stop, I will. Say the word and we will both put our clothes back on."

"No." She wanted him, and this. If they were going to be married, it would be a part of their lives. She needed to let go of her fear. He'd given her nothing but pleasure thus far, and the first time, so she'd been told, was usually unpleasant. He was trying to make it easier for her, and she trusted him. "I want you. Don't stop."

Slowly, he started to enter her. She froze momentarily at the slight pain, but the pressure started to feel nice, almost right even, mixed with the pain. This wasn't as bad as she thought it would be. She might even like it a little bit.

"I'm inside," he gritted the words out. "Are you all right?"

She loved him so much. He wanted to do right by

her. How could she not want to spend the rest of her life with him? "I am," she reassured him, and brushed her hands over his hair. "Please…I need you to continue." She moved against him, almost sensing there was more, and she wanted whatever it was.

"Thank God," he said. His patience was infinite. He kissed her over and over as he rocked into her. When she reached her climax, it was powerful, and she lost all ability to think for several heartbeats. Rhys reached his peak soon after, and she couldn't recall ever feeling this content. This was what she'd needed…Rhys, only Rhys. She'd always choose him.

EPILOGUE

One month later...

Rhys stared at his wife. They had been married a sennight, and he still couldn't believe she was his. He'd always considered her to be, but never thought she would marry him. They'd sparred often throughout their lives, and sometimes they still did, but they always ended up naked and writhing with passion afterward. It was a much more pleasant way to settle an argument.

They'd had the banns read immediately so they could marry in three weeks' time, and their wedding had been held at Weston Manor. Her father and brother had made the trip to attend since the rest of their family had already been in attendance. The house party had been extended and turned into a wedding celebration. Everyone had been excited for them. Of course, they had lied and told everyone they'd been secretly engaged a while. It seemed to be better than the truth.

"Are you sure you won't mind giving up your dream to be a spy like your father?" she asked.

"I'm still working for the home office," he told her. "I don't need to go anywhere to help my country." Rhys kissed her nose. "This is exactly where I want to be. You're my life and the only dream I could ever hope for. Though it wouldn't hurt to have children one day."

"I'd like that too," she said and then smiled. "I'd prefer that it is only the two of us for now."

"Me too," he agreed. Rhys wanted to have children, but he found he enjoyed spending time with her. They were acclimating to a lot of change, and most of it was good. He didn't want to share her with anyone. He loved being able to have all her attention. Any children they had would change the dynamic of their relationship. They needed time to discover who they were as husband and wife before they brought any babies into the world.

"I love you," she said.

"Are you certain?" He lifted a brow. "There was a time you hated me."

"I loved you then too," she admitted. "I didn't want to admit it, but it has always been there."

Some things were undeniable, and their love was one of them. He couldn't imagine a different life. He was meant to love her, and he would ensure that she always knew how much he adored her. Rhys leaned down and kissed her, allowing the rest of the world to fade away…

Thank you so much for taking the time to read my book.

Your opinion matters!

Please take a moment to review this book on your favorite review site and share your opinion with fellow readers.

www.authordawnbrower.com

EXCERPT: SHOCKED BY MY VIXEN

BLUESTOCKINGS DEFYING ROGUES BOOK FOURTEEN

DAWN BROWER

USA TODAY BESTSELLING AUTHOR
DAWN BROWER
SHOCKED
BY
MY
Vixen
Linked Across Time

Summer 1835

Scarlett stared out the window of the library at Weston Manor. She shouldn't be there. Not the library, the Weston estate… Something inside her told her she'd regret allowing her mother to bring her there. Her premonitions never steered her wrong. Not once since she realized she could sometimes predict the future. She may only be five and ten, but her otherness often made her feel ancient. This time was no different.

"Why are you in here alone?" a gentleman asked.

She turned to meet Christian Kendall, the Marquess of Blackthorn's gaze. He was a couple years older than her and he remained a complete gentleman. That might be because this was his family home, and one day he'd be the duke, or it could be his demeanor. She wasn't certain either way, or why it mattered to her at all. Scarlett shrugged nonchalantly. "There's nothing of interest outside this room."

Christian, she couldn't think of him as Lord Blackthorn, it seemed to impersonal and formal, tilted his head to the side. "But there's something entertaining in here?"

"Of course," she replied and gestured toward the shelves. "There are numerous stories on the shelves that could take me to different worlds anytime I choose."

He smiled. "I suppose that is true." Christian moves closer to her. "Do you have a favorite book?"

She shook her head. "I'd like to read some of the books my mother speaks of," she began. "You know from her time."

Christian's smile fell. Did he not like to speak about time travel? His mother, Alys, the Duchess of Weston, traveled from the same time as Scarlett's mother had. This was not a secret that either women had kept from their children. Scarlett had eavesdropped on several of their conversations over the years. They reminisced about how easy traveling was, mobile phones, and something called a hot shower. They all sounded interesting, but Scarlett doubted she would ever encounter them. She liked to think she was brave, but doubted she possessed the courage to travel to an unfamiliar time.

"I'm not sure I understand your meaning," Christian said carefully.

Scarlett shook her head and lifted up the corner of her lips. "Don't pretend you do not understand my words. It doesn't become you to play ignorant of our mother's pasts."

He lifted a brow, almost arrogantly. "We don't discuss these things. They're best left unsaid."

Scarlett sneered. He was a fool then. "Perhaps you should remind the ladies that brought us into this world of that fact. I do not believe they've received that particular message."

Christian sighed. "You're right of course." He stood in front of a large mirror and stared at his reflection. He was a rather handsome young man, and would probably become more gorgeous through the years. He wasn't for her though. She didn't know her future, but she did know she would not be a future duchess. That fate seemed atrocious and she refused to believe she'd fall in love with a man destined to thrust her in the middle of societal expectations. She would much rather do as she pleased without taking any of that into consideration.

"Do you know how time travel works?" he asked, still staring at the mirror.

"I do," she answered. "Well, not completely, I understand its possible, and that my family has certain gifts that allow us to bend time to our will. I don't know how they make it work."

Scarlett stared at the mirror. There was something unusual about it, and she was drawn to it. She wanted to touch it, but that meant moving closer to Christian. Before she realized what she was doing she had walked over to it and stood directly next to him. Their reflections staring back at them, almost taunting both her, and Christian, to reach out and what? Step inside? That didn't seem right. She closed her eyes and she could envision it. The two of them walking hand and hand right through that reflective glass.

"It's speaking to you too isn't it?" Christian asked in a hushed whisper. "It talks to me all the time and some days I almost want to give in to it."

Was that what it did? Spoke to those with abilities and lured them to the other side? Is that what had happened to her mother? Scarlett had never asked her how she'd travelled, and in turn, she'd never offered the details. Now she wanted to find out. Later, she'd finally ask her mother. She might volunteer the information on her own. Her mother's special gift was empathy and she could easily discern what bothered people. "It's doing something," she admitted. Scarlett reached for his hand and clasped in in her own. She didn't understand why she felt the need but didn't question it either. He glanced down at their hands, then met her gaze.

"If you wanted to hold my hand you should have said so sooner," he said in a flirtatious tone.

"Oh, do be quiet," she chastised him, then reached out and touched the mirror. Waves circled out as it would on a pond after a rock had been tossed in. She flinched at the soft texture not expecting it. "Did you see that?"

"I don't think you should do that again," Christian answered, his voice taut.

The waves cleared and an image formed in the mirror, it no longer showed their reflection. Instead it showed...their future. Scarlett hadn't expected that. An older version of them were in this very library in a passionate embrace. His hair was a little lighter, almost sun kissed, and hers...was a darker shade of red. He kissed her as if his life depended on it, and it did funny things to her insides. Sensations spread over her and she nearly groaned. Scarlett could almost feel what her future self did.

"That…" His voice was hoarse as he spoke. "That can't be true."

"No?" She turned to him and lifted a brow. "Do you find me that disgusting then?"

"I didn't say that," he replied defensive. He glanced down to their clasped hands and yanked his free. "It's…not that at all. The mirror must be bamming us."

"To what end?" She was disgusted with him. Scarlett wanted to jab him a few times and curse at him, but held back. He didn't deserve to breathe the same air as she did. "Are you suggesting the mirror is sentient?" She snorted. "Don't be ridiculous."

Scarlett turned away from him and started to leave the room, but stopped when he called back to her. "You can see the future, can you not? Do you honestly think that will happen?"

She kept her back straight and didn't turn to meet his gaze. His unworthiness was growing by leaps and bounds. Scarlett didn't speak about her gifts. How could he possibly know? "My future has nothing to do with you." After she spoke she continued out of the room. She didn't explain that she couldn't see her own future and had no way of ascertaining if the vision in the mirror was true or not, but she hoped it was as he said…a trick of some sort. She hated to think that she would desire him, and allow him to kiss her in that fashion.

Deep inside, though, she believed it to be true. Even when she wanted to deny it to her last breath. Scarlett wanted him, had always been drawn to him, but kept telling herself he wasn't for her. She would repeat that mantra until one day she actually believed it…

EXCERPT: WILL MY ROGUE LOVE ME TOMORROW

LINKED ACROSS TIME 15

DAWN BROWER

Will My Rogue Love Me Tomorrow

USA TODAY BESTSELLING AUTHOR

Dawn Brower

PROLOGUE

December 1865

Lady Adeline Carwyn stared out the window of the library at Whitewood Abbey. Snow fell from the sky in big fluffy flakes and landed on the ground in soft piles. The night sky was filled with flurries making the stars almost indistinguishable against the blinding white snowflakes. Still she stared, hoping a wishing star might make an appearance.

Because…she needed one.

She was tired of being unloved. All right that was a slight over-dramatization. Her family adored her. Her parents were the best a girl could have, and her grandparents were doting. Her little brother, annoying as he was, loved her too. But that wasn't the same as being in love. She was one and twenty, and had yet to feel anything resembling romantic love for a man. Adeline wanted what her parents, the Duke and Duchess of Whitewood, had. Perhaps that was too much to ask.

"What is so interesting outside?" her little brother, Jamie asked. He was nameD after their grandfather, James Kendall, the Duke of Weston. He was ten years her junior, and from what she understood, a complete surprise to both her parents. They thought they wouldn't have any more children.

"Nothing," she answered lightly. He was one and ten, and had the curiosity of any child. "The storm seems to be going strong. I hope it doesn't prevent anyone from visiting for Christmas." They were having a house party that would last until the new year. Two weeks with family and friends they hadn't seen in a while. She was looking forward to seeing her younger cousin, Francesca Kendall. Jamie would be excited to see their other cousins, Carter Kendall and Oliver Rossington. Both were younger than Adeline, but older than James, and like her little brother, the heirs to the title their fathers' held.

"It better not," he said mulishly. "Mother

promised we'd have a grand time with everyone, and even promised I could come to the Christmas ball."

"Really?" she said as she lifted a brow. "The entire night?

"No," he said and sighed. "I can only stay until the first dance, and after the tree is decorated."

They usually decorated the tree as a family, but this year her mother, Elizabeth, had decided to break with tradition. They were going to have a day of creating decorations for the tree, and then the night of the ball everyone would put their creations on it before the festivities began in truth. "That sounds more like what mother would agree to."

He wrinkled his nose. "I don't care to stay for dancing anyway. That's something girls like."

"Oh," she began. "I don't know about that. You might feel differently when you're older. Some gentlemen enjoy dancing very much." And some avoided it altogether…

"Not me," he replied stubbornly. "I'll never like it."

Adeline leaned down and ruffled his hair with her hands. They both had the same golden blond locks and blue eyes like their parents. Jamie was starting to look a lot like a younger version of their father, and Adeline favored her mother. No one would look at either of them and doubt who their parents were. "I believe you." Their father didn't care for dancing much either. He only gave in when their mother wished it. The duke would do anything for his duchess. Their love shined from them both and it made Adeline envious. She glanced back out the window, but no star dared to shoot across the sky. Perhaps she should make a wish anyway. It might still come true.

"Have fun staring out the window," Jamie said. "I'm going to do something productive."

"Such as?" she asked with curiosity.

"I'm whittling a few things for gifts. I have to finish the horse I'm making for grandpa." That was a brilliant idea. Adeline wished she had a similar skill so she could make something creative as a gift. Jamie was very talented, and it was part of his special abilities. He was tactile and got impressions from items after people touched them. Adeline, unfortunately, in her estimation was an empath. She felt too much and sometimes when she was around individuals their emotions became hers. It made socializing difficult, and also falling in love. It made her mistrust her own feelings.

"I can't wait to see them." She lifted her lips into an affable smile. "Go finish your gifts. I'm going to sit here a little while longer."

"I'll show you when I'm done," he promised, then skipped out of the room.

Adeline turned back to the window. The snow had lightened and wasn't blowing around as much. The sky was more visible, and the stars seemed to blink at her. She sighed. What did that mean? She decided not to question it any longer. There was no reason to keep waiting for a shooting star. It was an impossible expectation, and it didn't mean her wish would come true.

Instead of hoping for the impossible she closed her eyes and sent her hopes and dreams out into the world. She wanted love, even if it only existed for one night alone, it would be enough she promised.

It wasn't too much to ask, at least she prayed it wouldn't be. A handsome man who saw her, and not her father's title and fortune. Someone that would kiss her until she lost the ability to breathe, touch her as if she were irresistible, and speak sweet words to her until her heart beat rapidly inside her chest. A moment of love and a lifetime of memories. It would be enough. God, she hoped it would be…

Adeline opened her eyes and stared up at the sky. Nothing had changed outside, and she didn't feel any different inside. Maybe her wish had been for nothing, but she didn't think so. Guests should start arriving tomorrow, and perhaps, if her wish had been heard, it would include someone for her to love.

And maybe, his love would be real, and not generated by a wish from a fanciful lady desperate for something tangible.

EXCERPT: THE VIXEN IN RED

BLUESTOCKINGS DEFYING ROGUES BOOK
EIGHT

DAWN BROWER

USA TODAY
BESTSELLING AUTHOR
Dawn
Brower
The Vixen
in
Red

The sun was high in the sky and the wind blew lightly across Lady Charlotte Rossington's face. The garden at her father's, the Marquess of Seabrook's, London house had started to bloom. The flowers were mere buds, but they showed promise of being true beauties when they reached their peak. She reached down and brushed her fingers over the tiny buds and smiled.

"Are you certain this plan of yours is wise?" Her closest friend, Lady Pearyn Treedale asked. Her dark locks were pinned back into an intricate chignon, but a few tendrils had escaped in the breeze. Her blue eyes were the same shade as the sky. She was a true beauty and one day would be a duchess, if her fiancé ever deigned to return to England. Pear didn't mind his absence. She'd enjoyed being out in society without having to bother with finding a suitor. In some ways Charlotte envied her. She very much did not want to partake in any society events.

"It's the only way I can make my mother understand my wishes. Her only desire is to see me married and having babies." Charlotte wrinkled her nose in distaste. "I have more wants and desires than can be found in wedding vows and a lifetime of marriage. She may have found happiness with my father, but I would prefer to have much more than love to sustain me in my future." Maybe one day she wouldn't mind finding a man to give her heart to, but not for a long time. Charlotte wanted time to be alone, explore *who* she was deep inside, and write. She had so many ideas and she wanted to have time to put the stories inside her head down. Sharing those stories with the world was her greatest dream. She would not be able to do any of that if her mother forced her to participate in the season.

Pear took a deep breath. "I understand, I do, but I cannot help wishing there was a better way." She twisted her mouth into a frown. It was not a pretty look on such a lovely face. "The scandal…"

"Is the reason I'm doing it at all," she reminded her friend. "My mother won't have any choice. She'll have to let me return to Seabrook. There I can weather the scandal and I'll be left in peace to write my first novel. It will work, I know it will." Her mother, Rosanna, the Marchioness of Seabrook, would be livid.

"I still do not like it. With you at Seabrook I'll be left alone in London all season. I'll miss you." Pear sighed. "And with you in seclusion your mother will not have a house party as she usually does. The one at Weston Manor will also be off limits for you. This seems extreme. Is writing your book worth being without any social interactions for months?"

She nodded her head vigorously. "Yes, yes, and yes," Charlotte said. The very thought of being alone to write…it filled her heart with happiness. "It won't be so terrible. We can still write each other and I'll have my family. Well, mother and father. I'm not certain what Rhys will decide to do. He might spend time in London with his wife."

Before her brother Rhys, the Earl of Carrick had married Lady Hyacinth, Charlotte had been thrilled at the idea of attending balls, soirees, musicals, anything that involved society. Her young heart had seen it as an opportunity, and in some ways it had been. The first year had been wondrous. Until she thought she'd fallen in love, and the rogue broke her heart. She gave up on finding someone. It hurt too much when the gentleman of her dreams crushed her fragile heart. She'd much rather take control of her life, and this scandal was the first step.

Pear tapped her fingers on the bench she sat on as Charlotte paced the garden path near it. "I suppose you wish for me to accompany you on this endeavor of yours."

"I would like it if you would," she said. "It gives my statement credence." The ton would notice Charlotte either way, but with Pear they would also gain the attention of any gentleman that happened to be nearby. Considering her affianced state it drew them all to her side. They thought they might coax her in breaking her engagement. What they didn't understand was that she liked being engaged; however, Pear had no desire to actually be married. She didn't want love any more than Charlotte did.

"Very well," she agreed. "I'll be glad to assist you in ruining yourself." She sighed heavily. "It is all quite dramatic. I hope that the end result is as you hope. I would hate for this elaborate scheme to be for naught."

"So you have mentioned several times." Charlotte grinned. "You truly are the greatest friend a lady could have." Then she clapped her hands with excitement. "I cannot wait."

"I can," Pear said dryly. "Once this is done I'll not likely see you until Christmastide."

"Don't be sour," Charlotte chastised her. "It is unbecoming."

"Now you *sound* like your mother," Pear said distastefully. "I don't think you're as unalike as you claim."

They might have some similarities, but there were not many. "We don't even look much alike. My coloring is more like my father's." Her hair had the same golden hue as her father's but her eyes were a blue shade somewhere in-between her mother and father's. Even her brother favored their father in looks. It was odd that neither one of them looked much like their mother. "Mother has complained about that often enough. She once said that if she hadn't given birth to us she wouldn't have believed us to be her children. It was very crass of her to say aloud." She giggled. "Though to be fair we were being termagants at the time."

"I do not doubt that," Pear told her. "You can be quite the hellion from time to time." She narrowed her gaze. "After this they'll consider you more of a vixen. Are you prepared for all the negative gossip?"

She had thought long and hard about it. Charlotte wouldn't enjoy what some in society would openly say about her. Some of it might even…sting. "It won't be anything resembling enjoyment, but I do believe I can withstand even the harshest of criticisms." Most of which would come from her own mother's sharp tongue. "Once I'm back at Seabrook I won't be privy to it any longer. So I can pretend they aren't saying anything at all. I'll be peacefully writing and forgetting the scandal. I will be all right." She smiled at Pear. "I do appreciate your concern for my welfare."

"Since you are resigned," Pear began. "Then we should prepare for this scandal of yours. I'll have the stables prepare our horses. Meet me there after you've made your wardrobe adjustments."

"Perfect," Charlotte said. "I'll meet you in the stable in twenty minutes. It should not take me long. We need to be away from the house and in Hyde Park before my parent's return from their luncheon with the Duke and Duchess of Huntly."

"Shoo," Pear replied and waved her hands at her. "There isn't a moment to lose."

Charlotte sprinted to the house and ran up to her bedchamber. Once there she stripped her gown, chemise, and shift off. Then she proceeded to change into a pair of her brother's old breeches, linen shirt, waistcoat, and jacket. She had been lucky enough to locate an old pair of his riding boots as well. Charlotte let her hair down from the chignon and plaited it, then twisted it in a knot at her nape. Once her hair was secured she slid a gentleman's hat on top her head. If not for her bosom and curves she might have been mistaken for a man at first glance. Satisfied with her handiwork she rushed down the stairs; careful to ensure no one noticed her, then went out to the stable.

Pear was already seated on her horse, and a groomsman held the reins to Charlotte's mare. She didn't ask him for assistance mounting. Charlotte strode to the block and slid on to the horse herself. Breeches were so freeing! She would have to figure out ways to wear them more often. She could ride like a man and not worry over a sidesaddle. Charlotte had instructed Pear to request a regular saddle. She was glad to see the groom had followed her directions. She turned to Pear and asked, "Are you ready?"

"Are we taking a chaperone?"

"That would defeat the purpose don't you think?" She nibbled on her bottom lip. "Are you worried about your reputation?" Charlotte didn't want to cause her friend any harm.

"I will be all right either way," Pear told her. "I don't have to worry about securing a good match. I'm flush with funds and I even have a fiancé if he decides traveling the continent is boring and returns to England. I was uncertain how much of a scandal you wished to cause is all."

"Well if you don't mind…"

"I do not," Pear reassured Charlotte, then pressed a knee into the side of her horse and guided the mare into a walk. Charlotte did the same and then they started on their path to Hyde Park.

They did not converse for most of the trek to the park. Charlotte was too nervous to find words. So far everything had gone as planned. The rest had to follow suit. Otherwise the entire scheme would have been for nothing. She pressed her lips into a line as she anxiously rode beside Pear. Finally they reached the park and steered the horses to the correct path. Hyde Park was the place to be seen and a large portion of the ton showed up to walk or ride in the late afternoon. There were perhaps not as many in the park as usual, but that was in large because it was not yet the full season. Early in spring was still early for the Season, as the gentry would not start to fully return to town until May. Still, there was enough of the upper crust in Hyde Park for Charlotte's purpose.

"Are they all looking at us?" she said in a loud whisper to Pear.

"Oh, yes," she reassured her. "There are quite a few discussions, and a few pointed glances, and fingers in your direction.

She hated being the center of attention. Charlotte had never wanted to be the belle of the ball. It would be much more to her liking if she could dance a couple times, then retreat to the library. Occasionally a ball could be fun, but more often than not she'd hated them. "Good." The influx of gossipmongers would ensure that she would be at Seabrook by the end of the week…maybe sooner.

"You were right," Pear said. "Wearing men's clothing certainly caught their attention. Probably more than you anticipated." There was a bit of awe in her voice as she glanced around the park. "You still want to do one full round around the loop?"

"Yes," she said. "It has to be complete."

Though she was starting to wonder if she had lost her mind. The more they moved through the park the more the members of the ton started to talk…and loudly. She heard several unkind words she had wished she hadn't. Charlotte reminded herself that this had been what she wanted. It didn't hurt any less…

Finally they reached the end of the path and the exit to the park was in sight. She froze. Her parents were strolling into the park with the Duke and Duchess of Weston. Charlotte had not anticipated that outcome. She thought she'd have time to go home and change. Then let the gossip come to them. Her mother's eyes widened, and her father turned toward her. His eyes glittered with disappointment. That hurt more than the harsh words. She hated displeasing her father…

Charlotte swallowed hard and held her head high. The time for turning back had passed the moment she left the townhouse in men's breeches. She had done this on purpose and now she had to pay the price for it…whatever that may be.

ABOUT THE AUTHOR

USA TODAY Bestselling author, DAWN BROWER writes both historical and contemporary romance. There are always stories inside her head; she just never thought she could make them come to life. That creativity has finally found an outlet.

Growing up she was the only girl out of six children. She is a single mother of two teenage boys; there is never a dull moment in her life. Reading books is her favorite hobby and she loves all genres.

bookbub.com/authors/dawn-brower
facebook.com/AuthorDawnBrower
twitter.com/1DawnBrower
instagram.com/1DawnBrower

If It's Love (Amanda Mariel)

Odds of Love (Dawn Brower)

Believe In Love (Amanda Mariel)

Chance of Love (Dawn Brower)

Love and Holly (Amanda Mariel)

Love and Mistletoe (Dawn Brower

Bluestockings Defying Rogues

When An Earl Turns Wicked

A Lady Hoyden's Secret

One Wicked Kiss

Earl In Trouble

All the Ladies Love Coventry

One Less Scandalous Earl

Confessions of a Hellion

Coming Soon

The Vixen in Red

Marsden Descendants

Rebellious Angel

Tempting An American Princess

How to Kiss a Debutante

Loving an America Spy

Marsden Romances

A Flawed Jewel

A Crystal Angel

A Treasured Lily

A Sanguine Gem

A Hidden Ruby

A Discarded Pearl

Novak Springs

Cowgirl Fever

Dirty Proof

Unbridled Pursuit

Sensual Games

Christmas Temptation

Linked Across Time

Saved by My Blackguard

Searching for My Rogue

Seduction of My Rake

Surrendering to My Spy

Spellbound by My Charmer

Stolen by My Knave

Separated from My Love

Scheming with My Duke

Secluded with My Hellion

Coming Soon

Secrets of My Beloved

Spying on My Scoundrel

Shocked by My Vixen

Heart's Intent

One Heart to Give

Unveiled Hearts

Heart of the Moment

Kiss My Heart Goodbye

Heart in Waiting

Broken Curses

The Enchanted Princess

The Bespelled Knight

The Magical Hunt

Ever Beloved

Forever My Earl

Always My Viscount

Infinitely My Marquess

EternallyMyDuke

Kismet Bay

Once Upon a Christmas

New Year Revelation

All Things Valentine

Luck At First Sight

Endless Summer Days

A Witch's Charm

All Out of Gratitude

Christmas Ever After

For all my readers that love the Linked Across Time series. The last few books mean even more than I can say. I hope you enjoy them the end, and look forward to a new adventure, and new series to come, including a spinoff series titled Scandalous Gentlemen coming in 2021.

ACKNOWLEDGMENTS

This is where I thank my editor and cover artist, Victoria Miller profusely. She helps me more than I can ever say. I appreciate everything she does and that she pushes me to be better...do better. Thank you a thousand times over.

Also to Elizabeth Evans. Thank you for always being there for me and being my friend. You mean so much to me. Thanks isn't nearly enough, but it's all I have, so thank you my friend for being you.